CW01475689

The Servicing and Maintenance of Wayland Snowball

hadesgate

puBLicatioNs

Published by:
Hadesgate Publications
PO Box 167
Selby
YO8 4WP
Email: hadesgate@hotmail.co.uk

To Hanny

The Servicing and Maintenance of Wayland Snowball

Steve Dean

Best
wishes

Steve
Dean.

Mailings to: Steve Dean
                  c/o Hadesgate Publications
                  PO Box 167
                  Selby
                  North Yorkshire
                  YO8 4WP

                  www.hadesgate.co.uk
                  www.hadesgateforums.co.uk

ISBN 0-9550314-4-3

Cover design by Terry Cooper 2006

Prepared and printed by:
York Publishing Services Ltd
64 Hallfield Road
Layerthorpe
York
YO31 7ZQ
Tel: 01904 431213   Website: www.yps-publishing.co.uk

Dedicated with all my love to my wife and soul mate Kazz.
The only one who never doubted.

Acknowledgements

Many thanks to Garry Charles, for being in the right place at the right time.

Thanks to Paula Wilson-Buckle for literally everything. Thanks to David Pearce for allowing things to happen.

And special thanks to Ray Wilson, Web and Forum guru. A young man who proves that not all of today's youth are lost.

Chapter One

Who cares?

Clank.

"But what would you do with two women?"

Clank.

"Well, the same as you would with one."

Clank.

"I don't get it, if you've only got one ... thingy ... and there are two ... wotsits ... "

Clank!

Wayland put his bucket down heavily and looked at Marlo. "You do know what to do to a woman don't you?"

"Of course I do," wailed Marlo indignantly, "I've seen all those education videos you got off Two-book Tim. But they only showed one man and one woman. Where does the other woman go?"

Wayland sighed, "It doesn't really matter, on your face, on the first one's face, use your imagination!" He snatched up his bucket and crawled off down the narrow metal tunnel. Marlo sat back on his heels, brushing his head against the air vent roof. He was the taller of the two, about five feet ten in old money, slim of build, with slightly curly mousy brown hair and grey eyes. His overall appearance was one of a neglected building, still lived in but not completely functional. It was often said you could see someone moving about in there, but no one was answering the door.

An image had formed in his mind, a dull, flickering image, but when you have a dull, flickering brain what else can one expect? The picture was of a middle-aged woman sitting on Wayland's face. She was rather fat, fully clothed, complete with gloves and handbag, and looked a lot like his aunt Colin. Wayland's face was pressed almost flat underneath. Somehow, Marlo didn't find that at all erotic, except the bit about his aunt in gloves.

A curse of pain from up ahead dispelled the picture forever. Marlo grabbed his bucket and crawled towards the sound. Wayland had found another scrote, the strange, flattened creatures that did the job of rats on this planet. They had sharp spines under their greasy fur. Not being the brightest of animals, they crawled into the air conditioning vents and died of starvation, not even a scrote on its deathbed would consider eating another scrote. So they sat here and stank, well, they stank all the time, but more so when dead. When the resultant odour got too strong someone had to come up here and fish the bodies out. It was considered the worse job on the planet, usually reserved for punishment detail.

Wayland was nursing a cut on his finger, it was a tiny scratch, but men are martyrs to pain, being very sensitive souls. He was about five feet eight, but acted taller. His hair was black, almost jet. He wasn't conventionally handsome, in fact some said he was bloody ugly. This wasn't quite true, but he was no oil painting. Eyes of a dark brown and a slightly rounded, getting fat physique completed the description.

"That one was still alive," Wayland explained as Marlo emerged from the metallic gloom.

"Well, it isn't now. Look, its innards are now outards." Marlo peeled a long piece of scrote gut out of the grill where Wayland had thrown it. He wound the intestine around his finger, stretched it and swung it around, like he was playing with chewing gum, but even he wasn't stupid enough to put it in his mouth. After several minutes he finally got bored with it. Marlo retrieved the rest of the carcase, wiped its guts off the vent and threw it into his bucket.

"Why do they call him Two-book Tim anyway?" Asked Marlo.

"Because he's only got two books; The pop-up, scratch and sniff, wipe-clean version of the Kama Sutra, and the Bible. Takes them everywhere he goes. One dog-eared and worn, the other virtually brand new."

"Which is which?" Marlo wondered wide-eyed.

"Which do you think? you tit."

"Well, I don't know, perhaps he's very religious, perhaps he reads the Bible every night before going to sleep."

"It's not likely though is it? I mean, if he was religious what's he doing with the Kama Sutra?"

"Perhaps he's into Indian cookery in a big way."

Wayland sighed and shook his head, "We really are going to have to do something about your cherry aren't we?"

"I haven't got any fruit with me, but ... " Marlo stuttered to a halt under Wayland's glare.

"I think it's time for a break." Wayland decided. He unwrapped a long brown parcel from around his middle. "I borrowed this from the lab. Sonson told me it had certain medicinal properties." Wayland opened the parcel to reveal a leaf, which opened out to five feet from tip to stalk and about three feet across.

"What is it?" breathed Marlo.

"Ganja, man." replied Wayland in a totally unconvincing Jamaican accent. Marlo's shoulders sagged, "How the hell are we gonna make cakes up here?"

"What the f ... no, you dick-head, ganja, not ginger. You know, drugs! You smoke it. Look."

He pulled out a packet of cigarette papers, pulled one loose and replaced the pack. With a small penknife he cut off a section of the enormous leaf, rolled it up and wrapped the paper around it. After several attempts at lighting the green leaf it finally began to smoulder. Wayland sucked in the yellowish smoke. Apart from a coughing fit, nothing much seemed to happen.

"Yuck, that's horrible, wait 'till I get my hands on that Sonson." He stuffed the over-sized leaf into his scrote bucket and threw the smouldering dog-end on top. Wayland laid down on the cool metal of the ventilation shaft, light coming through the grill made a pattern of square shadows across his face. "I'm still having a break, got any of those bananas?"

"Yes, there are a few left." Marlo dug into the pocket of his stained pink overalls and pulled out a battered paper bag. In the bottom were a few of Wayland's favourite sweets, sugar bananas. They were yellow and vaguely banana shaped, there the similarity to any real fruit ended. Wayland ate the lot, then threw the empty bag into his bucket.

"What else could a man want?" sighed Wayland, continuing his earlier theme, "money, power, a big house, a nice fast sports car or three, a shit load of sugar bananas and two good looking women with big tits. Perfect. What have we got? A shaft full of scrotes!" He sighed deeply.

"I still don't understand why you need two women," Marlo laid down with his feet to Wayland's head. "From what I've heard you can't handle one."

"What! Who told you that!" Wayland shot upright, his head clanged into the roof of the vent. He laid back down nursing the top of his head.

"I read it on the wall in the ladies toilets on floor two."

"It's a lie, I can keep my end up with the best of … What were you doing in the ladies toilets?"

"I was looking for you." Replied Marlo.

"Anyway, that's not the point." Said Wayland ignoring the insult, "If I had two women to practice on I would be really good. Have you ever noticed how buckets are really sexy?"

A curl of yellowish smoke wafted down the vent, drifting on the lazy currents of the air-conditioning.

* * * *

A passenger in a space ship approaching the planet Greenshy would first see what would look like a green snooker ball on black felt. Here and there, as they got closer, long, thin lakes of greenish water would become visible. Closer still and the individual features would appear; tree clad mountains, forested valleys, rippling plains of lush grass. In short, sodding plants everywhere. Moving ever nearer, a cluster of buildings would come into view. The colony town called Pity. Being human dwellings they are naturally designed to fit in with the surroundings, so are a dull beige colour. Rose bushes, imported at great expense, fight a losing battle against the native plant-life.

When the planet was first discovered a message was sent back to base. Part of the message, a personal, fairly colourful comment by the mission commander, read 'I pity the poor bastards who will have to live on that green shyte hole'. However, the message didn't make it across the light-years intact, what finally arrived was 'Pity ... Green shyte ... ' Thus, with a little judicious pruning, a town was born.

In one of the buildings a small window reveals three people gathered around a desk, the important one sitting behind it, the other two, being more impotent than important, stand sheepishly before it.

* * * *

Wayland and Marlo stood in the manager's office. They were both attempting to look inconspicuous yet smartly efficient. They failed miserably. The manager, one Mr Hardstaff, was looking through a thick manila folder. The name Wayland Snowball was clearly stencilled on the front cover. Mr Hardstaff snorted through his large nose several times, closed the folder and fixed Wayland with his watery grey eyes.

"So, you're back again, the second time in the same week. That must be some kind of record."

Marlo smiled, "Oh great, I've always wanted to ... to, I never said a word," he faltered under the glare from Mr Hardstaff. He was a big man, wide shouldered and very muscular. Rumour had it that he broke a piece of the gym equipment by pulling too hard. The manager dropped the file onto his oversized desk. "Remind me, why is it you were in the ventilation system?"

Wayland mumbled and shuffled his feet. Marlo merely mumbled, he couldn't get the hang of doing two things at once.

"Come on, Wayland, surely you remember?"

He did indeed remember, it still turned his stomach when he thought about it. "We were on punishment duty, sir."

"Yes, but what for?" Mr Hardstaff intertwined his long, thin fingers, leaned back in his executive chair and waited.

* * * *

Two figures rolled along a darkened corridor in the middle of the night.

"Thsnotheway." slurred the first.

"Wha." Said the second, too drunk to even say the question mark.

"I say, this not the way to hour 'umble stablishmen'."

"Well whooz jumble stable mint is it the way to."

"Dunno, but if iz go' a bar itl do."

A door suddenly jumped out at them, stopping them in their tracks. The sign on the door read 'Mr A. Highcock, Assistant Manager.' But neither of the two were in any state to focus, never mind understand the importance of those words.

"This'll do, 'old don, were goin' nin." The door was unlocked, a big mistake around drunkards. Wayland fell in first, followed quickly by Marlo. Shushing each other loudly, they surveyed the office from their vantage point on the floor. Four blurry eyes saw nothing of interest until a light caught their eye. The pair managed to get into a crawling position and made their way over to the illuminated glass box. Two faces peered into an aquarium.

"Wa's at then? Look slike a fish ina tin." said Wayland.

"Tha's one a them te-pins. Like a toytoyse only they cun 'old their bref."

"Tha's clever. I woulda givenun you one athem fu yu burfday if I'd known."

"Tha's real nice fort tha' is. But you got me tha colander wi' them wimins on it wiv big carumbas."

"I'll get ya' one nesyear, I promis'."

Marlo smiled dreamily, then suddenly grinned widely. "Jew know wha' Te-pin means?"

Wayland, at a pivotal moment in his life, rushed blindly down the path marked 'Oh shit'. "I have no idea wha' it means, please do tell."

"Is a old red ingin word meaning 'edible'."

* * * *

Mr Hardstaff suppressed a smile. "But that's nothing to your latest escapade. I can't believe even a brainless moron like you would light a fire in a ventilation duct in the residential block."

"I don't remember any ducks," whispered Marlo.

Mr Hardstaff ignored him, continuing, "not just an ordinary fire though was it? Oh no, you have to go one better and light up a five-foot spliff."

"I didn't realise it had lit sir, the dog-end must have been smouldering when I put the paper bag in the bucket, which caught fire … "

"I am not in the slightest amount interested in the whys and wherefores of the deed. The fact remains that once again the assistant manager has had to suffer the consequences of your actions."

Wayland began to bite down on the inside of his mouth to stop himself from laughing, he had heard what had happened to Mr Highcock's wife, and the resident Vet who had been treating Mrs Highcock's tabby cat. According to his sources, the first outlet the smoke had gone down was the one nearest the Highcock flat.

"Mr Sidebotham, the Veterinary surgeon, performed an emergency caesarean section on Mrs Highcock's rare Classic Tabby British Short hair cat, under the influence of that damn drug." Mr Hardstaff was shouting now, to keep the smirk off his own face.

"I'm really sorry sir, I didn't realise the cat was

pregnant." said Wayland, trying to sound sympathetic.

"Not only was the cat not pregnant, it also wasn't female. He's shut himself in the family microwave oven and refuses to come out, even to have his tummy tickled, which is his favourite thing in the world according to Mrs Highcock."

"This brings us neatly to the lady herself, who was found unconscious on the kitchen floor, stark naked, clutching a cucumber in one hand, a bottle of sunflower oil in the other and a wide grin plastered across her face." Mr Hardstaff had to turn away this time, the image made even his tough exterior crack.

Wayland and Marlo stood very quiet until the manager turned back. "There were other reported incidents, most of them minor. Some of the residents actually asked for the 'air-freshener' to be injected into the system again. They said it made them feel relaxed. Now, Mr Highcock has asked that you be punished very severely, his actual words were 'wring the living shit out of the little turds'. Unfortunately, although this colony is run along military lines, we are not in the army, so I can't have you shot. I can, however, punish you according to union guide-lines."

Wayland smiled inside, which is a neat trick. He knew that the worst punishment was to clean the scrotes from the shafts, and they had already done that. As if reading his mind the manager spoke again. "I know you think cleaning the vents was bad enough, but I've discovered another, much more fiendish punishment for the two of you." With some considerable effort he pulled two stacks of computer printout almost a foot thick from one of his desk draws. "Stocktaking," he said triumphantly, dropping one in front of each of them with a satisfying thud!

Wayland groaned, Marlo seemed deep in thought.

"You, Snowball, will start at 'A', you, Brandon, will start at 'Z'. When you meet in the middle you may consider yourselves punished."

"But sir, I thought we had computers and robots and things to handle the stores, hardly anyone ever goes in there now." Complained Wayland.

"True, but it is a legal requirement that once a year a real live human checks the stock, we can't spare any, so you two will have to do. Besides, being away from people might do you good."

"But sir, that warehouse contains everything needed to run this entire colony, that must be millions of items, it'll take years." Moaned Wayland.

"So get moving, the quicker you start, the quicker you will finish." Mr Hardstaff turned his attention to other matters.

"He was a painter wasn't he?" piped up Marlo.

Wayland and Mr Hardstaff turned in bewilderment towards Marlo.

"You know, that guy Caesarean."

Wayland batted him around the head to save Mr Hardstaff the trouble, and pushed him out of the door.

Chapter Two

Wayland was half way down page four, with another six hundred odd to do. He had been at the job almost three weeks now, and had hardly got anywhere. It didn't help that although the printout was alphabetical, the stock on the shelves wasn't. The items were stacked according to part numbers, which confused the hell out of Wayland. He was already bored out of his tiny mind, the thought of all those pages left almost made him cry.

Somewhere in this vast complex his only friend Marlo was doing the same. He had hoped they would meet, perhaps he could trick Marlo into doing all of the work, then he could skive off somewhere. But the warehouse was so big he didn't hold out much hope. He hadn't seen his friend since that first day, not even after work. His head hurt so much after all this concentrating that he was forced to go straight to his room and lie down.

Every morning at the sound of his alarm a dread crept over him. With increasing effort he dragged himself from his pit and slunk towards the warehouse. The covered walkway looked out over alien vegetation towards a yellow lake. The view was interesting if a little bright for his liking, but it was this that kept him going. Dreaming of one day being free of all this, of one day being manager himself and playing golf all day.

The present manager, and one whose position was not under much threat from Wayland, stood beside the door as he did every morning, checking Wayland was doing as he was told. He never spoke, just smiled knowingly and held the door open. Marlo, who entered from the other side, missed out on this daily treat. Mr Hardstaff didn't have the time to reach the other side of the large building. Wayland often wondered why the manager singled him out. It was very unfair.

So Wayland would turn to the last item with a tick next to it and start again. Walking down endless parallel rows of shelves ten metres high, climbing ladders, risking his life. And for what? Just to count tubes of anal cream and packets of asymmetric screws.

Every so often one of the robot shelf stackers would come whizzing down, forcing Wayland to run for cover. They were supposed to be human friendly but Wayland didn't trust anything mechanical around here. They did keep him alert though, at least most of the time. But this job was so mind numbingly boring only someone completely brain-dead could do it for any length of time. He had tried finding an empty shelf and sleeping, but the warehouse made strange noises when he closed his eyes, as though something was teasing him, so he had to give that up.

Half way through a typically boring day when not even the shelf stackers attacked him, an unusual noise somewhere up ahead and to his left made Wayland stop. Listening carefully he was sure he could hear voices. In the vain hope that it was Marlo talking to himself he ran towards the noise. As he neared he was disappointed to hear that the voices were female. Realising what this could mean, his disappointment turned to hope and he doubled his speed.

His silicon soled shoes trotted quietly down one of the long rows of shelves. The voices had stopped. When they started again he realised he had gone too far and began to back-track. A flash of orange as something moved told him he was in the right place. Peering through the stacked shelves he could make out a young woman, dressed in the regulation orange overalls of a techy. She was leaning provocatively against a large packing crate. She had long blonde hair, green eyes and was very pretty. By moving his head slightly he could see the other person, also a woman, but dressed in a blue business suit. She was obviously older by six or seven years, also quite pretty but a little stern looking. Quietly Wayland moved a few of the tins in front of him so he could see them both.

The two women were talking quietly, almost whispering. By pressing close to the shelf he hoped to hear better, but without being discovered, then if things worked out he could attract their attention. Two women would certainly make this job more enjoyable. To Wayland's infinite surprise the one in the suit leaned forward and began to undo the overalls of the younger one. The baggy orange garment opened to reveal a shapely chest supported by a white bra. The suit ran her hands over the breasts until they met in the middle, her fingers working at the material.

Wayland was amazed when the bra popped open from the front. What will they think of next he thought to himself. The suit pulled the cups aside, revealing firm breasts with small nipples. The younger woman meanwhile was opening the blouse and skirt the older one wore.

It's a well known fact to most people, women especially, that men have hollow spines. This has nothing to do with weight-to-strength ratios or an indication of the lack of courage. The hollow is there to allow the man's brain, when it turns to jelly, to slip down into his pelvis. It isn't known how, or even if, the reverse process works. This jelly effect can be seen in action by studying men in the presence of a woman with a large cleavage, a see-through top, or a pair of shorts so far up her crack it's a wonder she can walk. The speed of the brain-to-jelly transformation is speeded up in the presence of 'mates' and slowed almost to a stand still in the presence of mother-in-laws and wives with large biceps.

Wayland's jelly effect kicked in quite fast. He leaned most of his weight against the shelf, his eyes flicking between the four brown nipples. The orange overall slipped to the floor revealing tiny white knickers. The suit leaned back to admire them, probably a gift from her. Wayland's member throbbed harder as the young woman turned, exposing tight buttocks, the tiny panties disappearing between them.

The rising organ between Wayland's legs pushed against a jar of extra thick chunky-chilli relish on the shelf at crotch height. The jar pushed against another, which swivelled around a third, sending it crashing to the floor. The sound of breaking glass echoed around the virtually silent warehouse. Wayland froze in horror. The suit pulled her blouse together and rushed over to the shelf. Behind, the orange overalls quickly covered the exotic underwear.

The suit shouted, "Who's there? Who's that spying on us? Is it that pervert Mr Highcock again?" The woman was reaching through the shelf clearing a way to get a better look. Wayland did the only thing a man could do in these circumstances. He ran for it.

"Quick, he's running away, after him." A voice shouted.

As quick as he could, Wayland pelted down the row, hoping that a junction would come up on his side soon, one that would take him away from the two women. He dragged his bulk along the row, his feet hurting on the concrete floor. Wayland was too young to have a beer gut, his stomach was rounded because of his glands, he would say. It ran in the family, which is more than could be said for Wayland, who needed a lift to turn out his bedside light.

The sound of pursuing voices was close now, despite his head start and obvious male superiority. Suddenly up ahead he could see a junction, a gap between almost endless shelves to allow the robots to move from lane to lane. He rounded the corner just ahead of the voices, and ran straight into a shelf-stacking robot. His head bounced off a wooden pallet the robot was carrying, sending him staggering backwards.

"Caution," said the robot, "warning, danger, heavy machinery. Stand aside." The robot kept on, not waiting for him to move. Dizzily, he lurched backwards, stepped into a row and watched the robot slide past.

"Bloody things, I thought they had detectors and things." He said to its retreating back.

"You would of thought so." Said a voice behind him.

Wayland spun around, making his head hurt. The two women, now decently dressed stood before him, arms folded over their lovely chests. Wayland dragged his eyes away, tried to look at their faces. A pink blur shot out from the dark suit, a fist smashed into his gut doubling him over, toppling him to the floor in surprise. "We'll teach you to spy on us you pervert, is that how you get your kicks?"

Wayland was incensed, knocked to the floor by a woman! He leapt up, anger keeping him upright. "I don't hit girls, so think yourselves lucky, now go on, before I change my mind."

The woman in orange overalls stepped forward and belted him in the eye with a satisfying crack.

"Right, that's enough, if you want to fight, you got it." Wayland lifted up on his toes like he'd seen all the best kick boxers do. He'd watched plenty of martial arts films, he knew what to do. Skill-lessly, he skipped towards the suit and aimed a punch at her face. She dodged easily, grabbed his arm and twisted, forcing him down. At the same time her foot came sharply up and connected with full force against his genitals, squashing his nuts against his pelvic bone. Despite what you see in the movies, a man, once kicked in the knackers is good for nothing for several days.

Wayland clamped his hands over his crotch without touching the offended articles, then, slowly, very slowly, he collapsed to the floor. The next few minutes passed in agony, he was vaguely aware of being verbally abused and laughed at. Then all was quiet. In the eerie silence he could hear the beating of his heart, he cursed every thump as his balls throbbed with pain.

An hour later he was still there, huddled in a heap, thinking how god must be a woman to put these things on the outside. He had read once that birds and reptiles have their gonads on the inside. Why can't we? Wayland made himself a promise, as soon as he was rich enough he was going to have surgery, have them tucked up inside out of the way.

After another hour or so he was able to stretch out, then to stand up. Walking like he'd crapped himself, Wayland made his way back to the Catering section; condiments and relishes. A small robot like a metal dog with a wide mouth had just finished cleaning up the smashed jar. The robot turned towards him at his approach. "One jar of Chilli relish will be charged to your salary, do not let it happen again," it said in a reedy voice.

"Oh piss off you over-grown dildo, I'm not in the mood." Replied Wayland caustically.

"There is no need for that tone young man, it won't make matters any better." The machine added.

Wayland stepped forwards and kicked the robot square in its low face. He had the satisfaction of seeing several bits bend or fly off. Unfortunately, the robot turned out to be quite hard, being made of metal. A sharp pain ran through his toe, up his leg and bit his already tender testicles. Ouching loudly he slumped back onto an empty shelf, vowing not to move for at least a week. The small robot gathered up its displaced parts and trundled off shouting "Mechanic, mechanic."

Back in his room later he stripped and inspected the damage. A lovely purple eye had developed, swelling it almost closed. There was a fist shaped bruise on his gut, his ribs and backside ached, and he had been frightened to death when he'd pee'd blood. His scrotum had gone a lovely black colour and had swelled up, he tried not to look, but his eyes were constantly drawn back to the fascinating sight. And to cap it all, his toe was bloodied where he had kicked the robot.

"Shit, shit, shit!" He shouted eloquently, it didn't help.

So he tried having a shower instead, which did make him feel a little better. Afterwards, he laid on his bed, legs apart and a packet of frozen mange-tout on his knackers. The existence of this particularly delightful way of eating peas had completely passed him by until now, but he doubted he would be able to eat any after this.

The next morning, ritual psyche session over with, he stepped out into the corridor. Almost immediately the intercom crackled, "Wayland Snowball to the managers office, Wayland Snowball." There was the usual titter whenever his name was mentioned, then the speaker fell silent. Wayland was ecstatic. Could this mean the manager had finally decided enough was enough? No more stocktaking! The thought filled him with such joy he almost forgot his nuts were on fire.

The joy soon turned to despair when he stepped into the manager's outer office. The two women from the warehouse were sat primly on chairs just outside the inner door, obviously first in the queue to tell their story. They were both dressed in suits today, the younger one looking a little uncomfortable in hers. But they both looked really shag-able thought Wayland, in better days of course, when the swelling had gone down. He sat opposite the two and smiled when they looked his way. Not surprisingly, they returned only frosty glares.

The inner door opened and the frame filling bulk of Mr Hardstaff appeared. "Right ladies, if you would like to come in." He smiled his most charming smile. Turning to Wayland his smiled dropped instantly into a scowl. The door closed firmly behind the manager, leaving Wayland in a sweat in the waiting room.

What seemed a very long time later the door opened again and the two women trotted out. Looking down their noses at Wayland, they walked out of the door and disappeared. "You, in here." Mr Hardstaff said simply. Wayland stood and walked slowly into the lion's den, legs akimbo.

"I don't want to hear a word, before you start, the two ladies have told me all that happened and I naturally believe everything they say. Wayland Snowball does it again. I don't believe you, I really don't." Mr Hardstaff leaned back in his chair, which creaked alarmingly. He steepled his fingers, looked Wayland straight in the eye. "You're on punishment detail, you mess up, get put on further punishment detail and mess up again. What is your problem?" He asked metaphorically.

Wayland, who didn't know what meta-bollok-thingy meant, was thinking up an answer when the manager continued. "I have had enough of this. How long before you screw up big time and kill somebody? As manager of this place I have responsibilities. To the staff and the shareholders, who have invested heavily in this venture. I have no option but to transfer you."

Wayland looked up, a look of pure terror on his face. The transfer certainly wouldn't be somewhere nice. Like the spaceport, where all the exciting things happened, or the main admin block, where the crumpet was three deep. The only other place was ...

"So, as from nine am the day after tomorrow you will officially work for the department of alien flora testing."

The arsehole of the planet. If seen from space the various department buildings and locations were spread across the continent in the rough shape of a human body, D.A.F.T was slap between the legs, were the sphincter should be.

"Sir, no, that place is dangerous. Everyone knows about that alien fungus that feeds on human nipples. And what about that time when that scientist was killed?"

"Those are only rumours Snowball, blown up out of all proportion. That man had no right doing what he did to the melon-tree. Besides, that was a long time ago, I'm sure things are all under control now."

"But sir you can't send me there." Wayland snivelled.

"Can't Snowball? What grade are you boy?" Snarled Hardstaff.

"Er, c.a. sir," mumbled Wayland, looking at the floor.

"Exactly, clerical assistant. In the scheme of things, where does a clerical assistant figure?"

"Lower than whale shit, sir."

"Exactly, lower than a particularly deep whale's shit. The only thing lower than clerical assistant is office junior, and we don't have any of those do we?" Mr Hardstaff demanded.

"No sir," sighed Wayland, not enjoying this one bit.

"Right, now, I'll give you the rest of your time here to pack and to say goodbye to your friends ... friend. He will be staying here."

Wayland looked up in surprise, Marlo, staying here? What would he do on his own?

"Yes, that's right, Marlo has expressed a wish to be moved to warehouse duties permanently, he says he really feels at home there. As you won't be here to lead him astray I have agreed. Although it isn't strictly necessary. The computer system can handle all that perfectly well." Catching the look on Wayland's face he said, "Yes, that's right, I lied. All that stocktaking you did was completely unnecessary. Any problem with that?"

"No sir." Said Wayland through gritted teeth.

"Right, off you go then, I would come and see you off, but you know how it is."

Wayland turned towards the door. "Oh, by the way," added Mr Hardstaff, "What is that bulge in your trousers?"

"Mange-tout, sir." Wayland answered.

"Oh, carry on then." The manager turned back to his desk.

Chapter Three

Oh, sh ...

"Beer."

"Check."

"Women."

"Naturally."

"Trifle."

"Trifle ... Trifle? We don't want bloody trifle."

Wayland and Marlo were writing out a list of needs for Wayland's farewell party. Marlo was tapping on the keyboard of a word-processor as they talked.

"But I like trifle, made with real strawberries and proper cream."

"Ok Trifle."

Marlo grinned broadly and typed 'tryfl e' on the crumb-encrusted keyboard.

"We need to spread the word as well. Once this list is entered in we can add a few party graphics and turn it into a poster, then E-mail it to everybody on base. We can have the party in one of the canteens, then we will have plenty of room for all the chicks."

"What kind? Fried or roast?"

"Fried or roast what?"

"Chicken."

"Are you deaf as well as thick? I said chicks, you know; totty, fluff, willy-warmers, women. I'm going to get you laid tonight if it's the last thing I do. That should clear up your spots and help you concentrate more."

"Wow, that's great! Thanks Wayland, you really have been a friend to me." Said Marlo, admiration written across his big, stupid eyes.

"No problem, Marlo. Right, so how are we getting on?"

"We're doing great. Now, if only I could work out how to use this computer … "

* * * *

The canteen was virtually standing room only later that night. In one corner a colourful banner which read 'Wayland Snowblals goin a way praty' had been stuck to the wall. Marlo was quite proud of his handiwork, it had only taken him three hours to make. The tricky bit had been the little bunny rabbits and turtles, but he'd managed it in the end. When Wayland saw it Marlo noticed he was too choked up to say anything, at least he had a strange expression on his face.

Beneath the banner Wayland sat silently, staring into a half-pint glass of beer. Marlo was tapping his hands on the table and swinging his shoulders. "Come on Wayland, get into the spirit of the occasion."

Wayland leaned forward and slammed his hand against Marlo's. "There's no music, and everybody else is here to see the base dentist's annual check-up and grisly museum road show. Nobody has even noticed me, I might as well not exist."

"Nonsense! Two-book Tim dropped by."

"Only to tell me to return his videos before I left or he'd turn my scrotum inside out with a claw hammer."

"Well, it's the thought that counts." Smiled Marlo brightly.

Wayland had often considered putting the annoying little twat out of his misery, but then he would have nobody to borrow money off.

A woman of about twenty broke from the dentist queue and approached the table. "Hello Wayland, so you're leaving us then. Where you headed?"

"Oh, er, over to er, to the spaceport, you know, promotion and all that." Wayland lied, badly.

"Best of luck then." She turned and disappeared into the crowd.

"Gagging for it!" shouted Marlo. "You were in there man, you could've had her over this table."

"I know, but where's the fun in that?" said Wayland, thinking of all the fun in it.

"Wow, you really are my hero, turning down sex like that. If anybody offered me sex, I'd never refuse. Hell, if there was somebody lying naked and unconscious on a bed I'd be in there, no messing." Marlo nodded, agreeing with himself.

"Well hopefully it won't come to that. Now eat your trifle and let's get moving."

"Do I have to eat all of it?" complained Marlo.

"Look, you wanted it, remember? So bloody well eat it."

"All right."

Several minutes later Marlo scrapped his bowl clean, then finished it off with his tongue. "Right, I'm ready. Let's go pop my strawberry."

"Cherry, lose your cherry, you pop a duck." corrected Wayland.

Marlo smiled, "Cor, sounds kinky."

"By the way, Wayland." Marlo added to Wayland's retreating back.

"Yeah, what?"

"Did you have to get a fifteen portion trifle? I feel a bit sick."

* * * *

Through the vastness of space, travelling the speed of light, going on forever, radio signals stream out from dear old mother earth. She leaks like an old man's bladder, sending radio and television programs to all with the need and the equipment to receive them. Due to a quirk of fate and several technical details you wouldn't understand, the programs reaching the colony of Pity on planet Greenshy were all from the seventies. Although more up-to-date programs were available via the Zip-link faster-than-light pay-to-view channels, most people preferred the more esoteric, and cheaper, radio wave stuff.

All this goes part way to explaining why Wayland and Marlo were dressed in flares. For those of you too young to remember, imagine normal trousers that, on reaching the knee, suddenly took off at an angle to resemble a small campsite around the ankles. It didn't stop there though. Wayland was also wearing a ginger and pink striped tank top, a shirt with ten inch (twenty five centimetre) collars covered in printed blackberries, and purple shoes with two inch (five centimetre) crepe soles.

Marlo was similarly attired, but with small hedgehogs on his shirt, and his tank top was ginger and red. Fortunately for all involved, regulations didn't allow bubble perms or medallions the size of dinner plates. Very few people, either in the colony or back in the real seventies, were able to dress in the fashions of the time without looking like an explosion in a curtain shop. Wayland and Marlo were no exception. And, by no means alone in their choice of clothing, they still looked particularly silly. So, dressed like dicks and feeling a million dollars, Wayland and Marlo went 'on the pull'.

* * * *

Slap!

"What did I do wrong?" Cried Marlo, rubbing his sore cheek.

"Did you say what I told you to say?" Asked Wayland.

"Of course I did, I walked casually over to her and said 'Hello darling, do you ride bareback?' Perfectly reasonable question."

"Yeah, just your luck to go and pick the only frigid lesbian in the place. Look, there's another one, use my other best chat up line this time." Wayland pointed to a rather large boned girl wandering away from the dental booth.

Marlo homed in like a well-trained spaniel.

Slap!

This time Marlo nearly lost his footing as he was spun right around by the impact. He stumbled back to Wayland, who stood propping up the bar. A livid red mark in the shape of a fat hand covered one half of Marlo's face. "I don't believe my luck tonight, two frigid lesbians in the same hour."

"I don't understand it, these chat up lines are guaranteed to work. You did use the right one?"

"Yep! I walked right up to her and said, plain as day, 'You don't sweat much for a fat lass,' then smiled like you said. She looked me up and down, then BAM! Out of nowhere. I don't think I can take much more of this, isn't there another way?" Marlo slumped onto a bar stool and took a long drink of beer.

"Look, I didn't really want to do this, I think you deserve better, but we'll just have to go visit Sheila. She's a bit of an old slapper, but it looks like her or nothing."

"Who's Sheila? Don't think I've ever heard of her."

"That's not her real name, it's just a nick-name, Sheila Blige. You'll have no problems with her."

Half an hour and a couple more drinks later, their courage had risen sufficiently for them to attempt a visit to Sheila's.

Half an hour after they were back. "On leave? I can't believe she's on leave. I only saw her this afternoon, up against a filing cabinet with Bargepole Joe. Well, she was against the filing cabinet, he was by the photocopier. She must have got one of those last minute jobs."

"Yeah, up against the filing cabinet," said Marlo despondently.

"That leaves us with no alternative, If you want to go home tonight without that fruit basket around your genitals it's got to be Deborah."

"Deborah? Is that a nick-name too?" said Marlo around his glass.

"No, that's her real name. Some people call her Dartboard Deb," explained Wayland.

"Why?" Asked Marlo in all innocence.

"Because she ... likes to play darts. But never mind about that, let's just go see if she's in."

Half an hour later they were back. They had switched to shorts now, were passed merry and on the way to pissed as farts.

"A queue, I don't believe there was a queue. And a sign by the stairs, 'Queuing time two hours from here.' That women must be a nanimal." Marlo groaned into his empty glass. "Celebrate, tha's what I'm going to do."

"Celebrate what? Being the oldest virgin in Pity?"

"No, you mis-construct. You know, not have sex."

Wayland thought for a moment then said, "I think you mean celibate."

"I though' tha' was a bone." Marlo slurred.

"No, it's not having a bone." Wayland grumbled. Although not a virgin himself, having had sex several times, not all of them on his own, it was quite a long time ago. He was hoping to dump Marlo on some poor unfortunate woman then go get some action himself. "Are there any blind women on the colony?" Wayland thought out loud. "Or perhaps you could go for something older. I've heard that middle-aged housewives can be grateful, but I don't think we have those here."

"I think I'll jus' av' another drink, make it a double." said Marlo loudly, swinging his glass at the barman.

They sat in silence for a while, then began the usual put the world to rights bullshit that drinkers talk. Marlo brightened as a woman entered the bar. She was slim but full breasted, and quite attractive. She walked towards them but veered off at the last minute, as though she wasn't wearing her glasses, so needed a closer look.

"Look at the tits on that." Shouted Marlo straight at her.

She smiled, half at the compliment and half at the state of the vocaliser.

"Seen 'em, felt 'em, sucked 'em, shagged 'em." Intoned Wayland, keeping up the bullshit flow.

"Wow! That must of been great." Marlo sighed.

"Yeah, she was all right, her mother was better, you know, more experienced."

Marlo's jaw dropped open, a look of complete adulation on his face. "Way, you're a real man, man. I salute you." He raised his glass, then knocked back the contents in one gulp.

The rest of the night faded into alcoholic oblivion, one drink following another, until pissed as farts turned into smashed as fucks.

* * * *

"We are having a little difficulty with your life this morning, meanwhile here's some music." A little voice said in Wayland's dream. The music went 'thump, thump, thump.' in his head. When he tried to open his eyes someone shone a really bright light into them. He tried to complain, but a scrote had crawled into his mouth and died.

After what seemed like several years he was finally able to peel up his eyelids and take stock. A quick check of his extremities revealed no missing limbs. A clutch test confirmed the presence of two testicles and a penis, bruised and a bit crusty, but still attached. He was naked, true, but at least he wasn't wearing a policewoman's uniform. He was in a bed, not a cell, no sign of handcuffs or furry animals, and no expensive looking objects immediately to hand. He wasn't covered in vomit, tattoos or sequins. There was no wail of distant sirens and he was fairly confident he was on the same planet. All in all not too bad a night then.

A slight aching between the legs caught his attention. On moving to investigate further he felt the weight of another person beside him. Ah! He brightened, laid at last. Then the moment of dread, the time just before you turn over to see who it is. He had woken up beside a real dog once, and a very rough looking woman another time. Slowly, cautiously so as not to wake the other person, easier to slip out if she proved to be a fat slag, he turned over.

It wasn't a fat slag.

It wasn't a dog.

It wasn't a woman.

It was Marlo.

Wayland propelled himself from the bed, straight up in the air, using one hand. His mind shut down, refusing to think of anything in case a certain image appeared. His stomach clenched like a vice to keep hold of last night's intake. An involuntary scream hissed quietly out of a dehydrated throat. Wayland landed in a sprawled heap, dragged himself out of the door and ran naked down the corridor back to his rooms. The lock on the door burst apart from the sheer terror of Wayland's entry. (No, don't say that word!) Leaping into the shower, he turned the water on before his feet touched the anti-slip floor and washed himself for four and a half hours. All the time Marlo's words rung in his ears "If there was somebody lying naked and unconscious on a bed I'd be in there, no messing."

When Marlo awoke he was surprised to find Wayland gone, and, on enquiring about him was told he had left for his new post without leaving a message. Marlo was touched, obviously Wayland wanted to spare him any embarrassing scenes on his departure. What a great friend, do anything for you.

Chapter Four

Hot and throbbing

"Chitty"

Wayland leaned his forehead against the shuttle window in a vain attempt to cool a throbbing headache.

"Chitty!"

The air conditioning in this old transfer shuttle wasn't working, making Wayland hot and sweaty. This didn't help his headache. A hand shook his shoulder, rattling his tender brain.

"Chitty, son, I need to see your travel chitty."

An old man of about thirty-five scowled down at him, obviously ready to eject him forcefully from the vehicle if the chitty wasn't produced. Wayland fished around in a pocket and eventually pulled out a battered, dog-eared, stained travel permit with a phone number written on it. The old man snatched it from his hand. "What the hell have you done to this? We haven't even left Pity yet." Shaking his head, the shuttle guard examined the pass, "Wayland U. Snowball," The guard laughed, "What kind of a name is that? And the initials, WUS, are you? Are you a Wus? What does the 'U' stand for? Uneducated, uncouth, unemployed, oh dear. Ay? Do you want me to turn the heating down? Don't want you melting before we get there." The guard bellowed with laughter. He looked at the pass one more time, then returned it to Wayland.

Wayland stuffed the permit back into a pocket and returned his head to the marginally less hot glass. Inside his brain a little man was running around shouting 'Wayland slept with Marlo, Wayland slept with Marlo'. Another little man with a large axe was chasing him shouting 'Shut up, shut up,' but was unable to catch him. The guard went around the other passengers, pointing at Wayland and laughing, most of them joined in.

He tried to ignore the guard, examining his surroundings to give himself something else to fill his mind. He was seated in the window seat on the right-hand side of the old shuttle. Another seat, thankfully empty, by his side. There was an aisle separating a similar arrangement on the other side. In all there were twenty seats, a cockpit up front and a very uninteresting storage compartment at the back. Wayland stopped himself as he was counting the windows, he didn't want to look like a shuttle-spotter.

Eventually the shuttle engines started and the ship got off the ground. Wayland inconspicuously stared at his fellow passengers, all nine of them. The five men were nothing special, he guessed he could probably fight them all. Of the four women, two were too old, being in their late thirties. One of the others was worth a shag, you wouldn't kick her out of bed for biting her toenails. The fourth was very attractive, definitely worth a second or even a third rogering. Wayland considered going and sitting next to her, but thought no, not here. He would wait until they got to the flora station.

Several hours later, after two stops to drop off passengers, Wayland was alone on the craft. The good-looking woman had got off at the 'Drugs for Off Planet Export' centre. The remaining shagable woman a stop later. Leaving a hot Wayland to continue his journey with just his throbbing head.

A crackley voice announced their arrival at D.A.F.T. and the shuttle began to descend, apparently into a thick jungle. Wayland tried to leap out of his seat to warn somebody and nearly castrated himself with his lap-belt. By the time he had extricated his body the shuttle had landed, dropping out of the sky with a stomach turning lurch. But the expected crash and sound of greenery being pulped to juice never came. Instead the shuttle landed on a solid platform surrounded by living creepers.

The door hissed open and Wayland stepped out, no one to see him off, no one to greet him. The shuttle roared, almost deafening him, then lumbered slowly into the green tinged sky. Wayland was left in an ocean of green, some of which was moving slowly towards him. "Great." he said aloud. "Absolutely fucking wonderful."

"It does rather take your breath away doesn't it?" A sharp, bald head appeared as a mass of the creepers slid aside. "You'll get used to it, though it still takes my breath away when I return from leave. Are these yours?" The man asked, pointing to the bags in Wayland's hands.

Wayland was surprised by the sudden appearance of the man, and by the stupid question, he managed to stutter, "Er, yes."

"Good, come on then, I'll show you around. My name's Ernest Shorthorn, but please call me Ernest. This is the way in, and also the way out, to and from the landing pad. Don't worry about these sensor vines, you'll get used to them." The thick green mass of vines moved aside as they walked down a slope towards a steel door marked 'IN'. After they had passed the vines closed over them, leaving the pair in dull green shade.

Ernest pulled the handle, which Wayland noticed was marked 'handle', and stepped through. He wasn't at all surprised to find the door marked 'OUT' on the other side. They were in a short, narrow corridor with metal walls. The ceiling was covered in light panels, illuminating the passage with a dull cream coloured light. On the floor were several thin painted lines in different colours. The walls were each marked 'WALL'.

"It really is easy to get around here, just follow the coloured lines to get where you need to be. As an example we need to go to the infirmary for your medical, so we follow the blue line. Don't worry, you'll get used to it." Ernest smiled broadly, then lead the way.

The dreaded word 'medical' had left Wayland in a panic. He had heard you could tell if someone had had (here his mind quickly supplied the word 'it', instead of the words anal sex.) Although regulations permitted the free practice of sex between consenting adults, whether of the same, opposite, both, neither, once-one-now-another gender, in singles or groups of up to three hundred (fire regulations prevented gatherings of a larger size.) Wayland was still paranoid of anyone finding out. He began to clench his buttocks as he walked, trying to work his sphincter muscle into a solid, water-tight grip. Although he wasn't aware of it, this made him mince rather alarmingly.

The blue line did indeed lead to the infirmary, which unsurprisingly was marked 'INFIRMARY' and 'IN AND OUT'. Ernest turned to Wayland, "Now, Doctor Crippen will give you your medical, then if you pass, will send you to your room. Then, the base manager, Ms Knightley, will want to see you. Goodbye for now." With a cheery wave he walked off.

Wayland knocked on the glass door and stepped in. Behind a small, cluttered desk sat a plump woman of about fifty. She was dressed in an old fashioned pink shell suit and was using an ink pen to write notes onto a small brown card. "Behind the screen, strip, and smear yourself with the stuff in the jar." She said without looking up. Wayland lowered his bags to the floor, then shuffled uncomfortably over to the screen. Once behind it he slowly undressed then screwed the lid off the glass jar which sat on a low shelf. The stuff was very sticky and smelt of raspberries. He dug his hand in and pulled out a big dollop. Carefully he began to work the cold substance over his chest. When it was fairly well spread he bent down for another hand full.

"By George, you've lost weight." said Dr Crippen.

Wayland straightened, his sticky hands over his genitals.

"Sorry young man, I was expecting my husband, Lionel. Wash that stuff off and come over here. Unless you want me to lick it off of course." She took a step closer, a gleam in her eyes.

"No! No, it's fine, honestly, it comes right off look." Wayland grabbed a wad of paper towels and began scraping off the jam.

"It's no trouble, but don't tell Lionel, he gets so jealous."

"Er, No I'm fine thanks, it's coming off a treat now." Wayland scrubbed the jam off as quickly as he could, he didn't want an old woman's mouth near him. With one last leer the doctor moved back to her desk. Wayland replaced most of his clothing, leaving his chest and his left arm bare. He presumed the good doctor would need to look at these bits, but she certainly wasn't seeing anything else. He sat down nervously, keeping her desk between them.

"Right," said Dr Crippen eagerly, "Let's get you sorted out. Name?"

"Wayland Snowball."

A slight smiled flicked across Dr Crippen's face. "Age?"

"Twenty three."

"Occupation?"

"Clerical Assistant."

"C.A. at your age? Shouldn't you be lower management by now?" The Doctor smiled openly this time.

"My manager doesn't like me, I've been held back." Explained Wayland.

"I've heard all about your exploits, young man. The one about the tom cat having a caesarean had us all laughing." She laughed again, as if to prove it. Wayland stayed silent, although his cheeks blushed slightly. The Doctor came round the desk and wrapped a piece of black cloth around his arm. Various wires trailed from it into a small computer in front of Dr Crippen. She looked at the box for a few seconds, then turned back to him. "Are you a virgin still? Or have you actually managed to dip your wick?"

Wayland turned deep crimson, "Of course I have, I am very active in that department."

The Doctor smiled widely, looked Wayland up and down and said, "Good, I like a man with experience."

"I thought doctors couldn't … you know … with their patients." Wayland stammered rather nervously. Dr Crippen leaned forward and squeezed his hand very softly. "But we haven't … you know … have we? Not yet at least."

Wayland leapt from the chair, throwing on his shirt

and fastening it wrong. "Well if that's all, I'll go now."

"Yes, that's all I can do to you at the moment," she sounded very disappointed, "Come again, any time, if you have any problems." She smiled a very sensuous smile for one so old, thought Wayland. Then he headed for the door.

Outside, as he was closing the door, a man slightly older than himself pushed his way in. He was tall, blond, wearing a white vest and shorts to show off his tan and large muscles. "Don't mind me," mumbled Wayland quietly.

"Ah, Lionel, at last, I've got something for you." He heard the doctor saying before he closed the door. He walked away with a look of disgust on his face. He suddenly remembered that the doctor was supposed to tell him where his room was. He didn't really want to go back into the surgery, he shuddered to think what they were up to in there. But it looked like he didn't have much choice, he had no idea where he was now or where he was supposed to be.

Quietly he walked back to the surgery. A strange sound filtered through the door, like someone trying to pump up an old football that was full of holes. Cautiously he opened the door and peered in. The noise was coming from behind the screen, accompanied by a kind of growling noise. "Er, Doctor Crippen, you where supposed to tell me where to go." He said rather timidly. The strange, wheezy noise stopped, then the doctor's head appeared around the edge of the screen, disappeared, then came back again. She spoke whilst her head was moving, "Just follow the red line, you're in room eighty two." As she smiled, waiting for his reaction, she was pushed forward so that her bare shoulders where visible. The biggest pair of breasts Wayland had ever seen swung out and back again. Out and back. His eyes locked on to them of their own accord, following the trajectory out of sight, predicting their position when they re-appeared. Wayland found to his horror that his trouser snake was firming up, preparing for lift-off.

The Doctor noticed his stare, "Would you like to watch? We can soon have this screen down. Lionel's a lovely mover, does my asthma the power of good." She laughed heartily.

"Er ... bimblemimblemumble." Said Wayland, closed the door rather quickly, and ran off along the red line. At what he considered a safe distance, he slowed to a fast walk. That was typical of my luck, thought Wayland. A women with tits that big, offering to lay it all open for me, and she's old enough to be my granny. I can certainly see why Lionel is interested, with those things swinging loose, and why he takes her from behind, it keeps that face out of sight.

The red line wandered around several corners, up some stairs, down some more stairs, and finally ran out in a short corridor. He had been trying to work out how many people must be based here, if he was in room eighty two. Perhaps some of them would prove as large as the Doctor but a lot younger, that would certainly give him one up on Mr Hardstaff.

He studied the door numbers as he walked down the narrow passage. The first number he found was seventeen. At first he thought he had a lot further to go, but the next door was number two. Puzzled, he crossed the corridor and examined some of the doors on that side. A livid green painted door was numbered sixty nine, the next threw him completely, reading merely 'room A'. Carrying on along he finally found a door with eighty two written on it, the numbers where so big he had to step back to read it properly. The black lettering virtually covered the entire door. In the space in the middle of the number eight was written 'DOOR'.

Wayland knocked on the door and went in. The room was very small, but antiseptically clean. Well, he'd soon change that, he had a pair of socks that would make an onion seller's eyes water. The room contained a set of bunk beds, two slim wardrobes, some kind of folding desk attached to the wall and a small stool. It was tastefully decorated in orange and blue, carpeted with twelve tiles, all grey and lit by a very bright light panel.

Wayland went over to the first wardrobe, might as well get settled in, he thought. When he opened the door he was startled to find it already full. Not just full, but packed, not a single space anywhere. The clothes were so close together that one garment couldn't be told from another. He tried the other one, which was empty. As he began to unpack, he realised why the other wardrobe had been so full. There was so little room in the damn thing it was full before half of his clothes were hung.

At the bottom of one of his bags, Wayland found the printout from the warehouse stocktake. No wonder his bag had seemed so heavy, he must have put that in there in his hurry to leave, after the ... after he'd had to leave quickly. He picked it up and examined the first page. Abalone paste, five crates of 24 jars; tick. Abba C.D.'s, 23; tick ... He tried to throw the thick wad across the room, even though the room was small the paper bulk didn't make it. Instead it landed on the bottom bunk where his feet would go. "Bugger it." He said loudly, then carried on unpacking.

Wayland went over to the desk and pulled it open, it folded down to quite a size, but had no room for any of his stuff. On looking closer at the bunks, he found the top one to be occupied. The bed was made like a sculpture, the sheets so tight you would have had difficulty getting a supermodel between them. There was a set of narrow shelves at the head of each bed, which Wayland threw some of his stuff on. The shelves on the top bunk were filled with books, all of which had their titles covered. Wayland tried to have a look but found they were jammed in so tight he couldn't pull them out.

Just then, a knock sounded at the door. Curiously, Wayland opened it. Ernest stood in the corridor, several feet from the door, "Are you in?" he asked.

"Yes, I'm just unpacking. Did you want me?"

"No, the base manager wishes to see you. So she says, but she probably wants to talk to you as well." Ernest grinned.

"All right, lead the way." Wayland said, closing the door.

"Oh, it's quite easy to find, just ask anybody."

Wayland looked around, there wasn't another soul for miles.

"How many people actually work here?" he asked.

"What here? Well, nobody really, it's just a corridor. Unless you count the caretaker robot." Answered Ernest seriously.

"No, I mean in the centre, in the whole building."

"Oh, it's not a building, you may have noticed it's all metal and has stairs everywhere. This is a space habitat, it was used by the first discovery mission as a base whilst they were in orbit. Then, when they decided it was safe to land, they came down in this until the colony was built."

"All right," breathed Wayland impatiently, "How many people work in this space habitat?"

"Well, I think they all do, but I must say a few of them seem to have a lot of spare time."

Wayland made fists with his hands to stop them going around Ernest's neck. He had a sudden thought, which got bored on it's own and wandered off. "If everybody who lives here got together at the same time, in the mess hall say, how many chairs would they need, if there was one each."

"Well, if the entire staff, including those on leave, sick leave, off duty, including management but not non-living workers, that would make about six and one for you."

"Seven! Seven people in a place this size, no wonder they needed lines to find their way around. "And of those seven how many of them stand up when they go to the bog, sorry, toilet."

"You have a strange way of putting things, but I think I know what you mean. There are four, now five, men and two women."

Ernest smiled in triumph. Good, thought Wayland, at least one other woman, odds are she's young, younger than the Doctor anyway.

Ernest led the way to the base manager's office. It was situated at the highest point in the structure, and actually had a window that wasn't obscured by foliage. The sign on the door read 'Ms Knightley, ass' manager.' Ernest knocked on the door then went in. "The new arrival Sonia." He smiled at Wayland then left.

"Come in, Wayland, come in." She walked around her neat desk and held out her hand. "Welcome to D.A.F.T. My name is Sonia Knightley, as you may have seen on the door. Call me Sonia, we don't stand on ceremony here. You may also have noticed that it says assistant manager. That's wrong actually, since the death of Mr Rogers, the previous manager, I have been promoted to manager myself, which is good isn't it? Now, sit down, then we can go over some base rules, all of which are designed with safety in mind."

Wayland looked Sonia up and down as she returned to her seat. She was about thirty, pushing it a bit, but she'd do if nothing better turned up. She was average to pretty, with nice brown eyes and a small nose. Her tits were a little small for Wayland's liking but still a couple of handfuls. She was dressed in a grey two-piece suit with a white blouse under it. A small silver brooch on her lapel was the only feminine item on her or in the room. At first he thought the brooch was a penis, but on closer inspection it turned out to be a space rocket of some kind.

She was listing the rules now, "One, don't go anywhere without reporting to someone first. It's literally a jungle out there." She laughed girlishly at her own word-play. "Two, if you go through a door that's open leave it open, if it's closed, close it, O.K? Sounds funny but it works. Three, don't touch anything without asking first." Wayland's eyes dropped to her breasts, damn, he thought. "Four, watch out for the plants in here, some of them get in from outside and can be dangerous, if you're not sure, ask. Five, no sex in the rooms, the walls are too thin, and those without sexual partners can get a little jealous. If you are going to do that sort of thing, either on your own or with somebody, go somewhere away from the habitat block."

Wayland had perked up at the mention of sex, but the matter-of-fact way she had said it was a right turn off. He also noticed her stressing of the words 'jealous' and 'that sort of thing.' Did this mean that Ms Knightley wasn't getting any? Or just mean she didn't want any? Wayland's shoulders slumped, he knew which one, if his luck was anything to go by.

Sonia continued. "I'll introduce you to everyone later, there aren't many of us here, but we are all a happy family." She grinned cheesily. "Has anyone told you what we actually do here."

"No … "

"Good, well I'll try to explain then," she interrupted. "Mostly we find, catalogue and do preliminary tests on native flora. Checking the plants for obvious commercial applications, new fruits, drugs, chemicals, that sort of thing. Of course the real work is done back in the main colony, but there are so many plants here, as you may have noticed," she snorted a laugh, "that we have to point them in the right direction, so to speak, in order for them to 'home in on' anything useful all the more quickly." She paused for breath. Wayland wasn't used to hearing such long sentences, he was beginning to lose concentration.

"You may be wondering where you fit into all this?" She gestured widely, taking in the office and the lush vegetation outside her window.

"Well … "

"I'll tell, you shall I? We need someone to keep records, file reports properly, keep in touch with base, that sort of thing. The day-to-day stuff that often gets over-looked but is vital," here she chopped her left palm with her open right hand, "to the long term, synergistic fecundity of this place."

Wayland could feel his brain going soft around the edges, if she didn't stop soon he would have an almighty headache.

"Lionel will be your immediate superior, giving you your daily tasks. But I will be asking you to perform for me from time to time. Have you ever worked under a woman before?"

"Er, no, I usually let them do all the work." Wayland was caught by surprise by her pause for his answer. Realising what he'd said, he blushed quite fiercely. Sonia seemed to either not notice or took it as a joke. She smiled, "you will find I'm quite fair, there is plenty of room for flexibility, on both sides of the desk."

Wayland glanced over the desk to her side, yes, there was room to bend her over the desk if she wanted him to.

Sonia stood and moved over to the door. "Now, off you go to the dining hall, I'll see you there. Just follow the yellow line until you find the green one, then follow that. See you later." Again she smiled, opened the door for him and closed it as he went through.

Later that night, the entire population of seven gathered in the dining hall, which seated ninety. One corner, near the automated meal dispenser, had been screened off. Ernest had declared himself host for the evening, taking it upon himself to introduce Wayland to the rest of the crew and to Ainsley, the meal making robot. Ernest walked around the assembled gang, touching each on the shoulder, "Now, this is Enid, Enid Crippen, doctor of medicine and doctor of botany. A rare person, you will agree, but very warm and friendly. Who, of course you've already met."

The Doctor winked openly at Wayland. Ernest moved over to stand behind Lionel. "This is Lionel Comely. Husband of the good doctor, and our science officer. A nice man, don't be fooled by all this muscle, really he's a big softy." Lionel leaned over and shook Wayland by the hand. His large, sweaty hand engulfed Wayland's, crushing his bones like clay. He looked deep into Wayland's eyes, then at his wife, then back to Wayland. No problem there thought Wayland, I wouldn't fuck her with yours.

Ernest had moved on, standing next to a rather short man, a few inches less than Wayland. He was in some kind of green uniform, not military, but not far off, consisting of a short sleeved shirt, plain trousers and black boots. All of which was spotless and immaculate. He looked to be about forty, solidly built, no monster like Lionel, but one to watch. His brown hair was cut short, brown eyes looked at you like they were measuring you up. He had a complete lack of distinguishing features; no face hair, no jewellery or tattoos visible, no scars or blemishes. Wayland had an uneasy feeling about the identity of his unknown bunk-mate.

"This is Sergeant Pettybone, base security. He also helps out with various other duties, he is a first class pilot and can fix almost anything that shoots a projectile." Wayland noticed that Ernest didn't touch Pettybone's shoulder like he did the rest.

Ernest walked over to the last man present, a tall, thin, dark-skinned man with a massive afro. He had his feet up on a chair and looked bored. The man flashed Wayland a bright smile, then returned to looking bored. "This is Sean O'Meara, assistant science officer. He also looks after the computers and robots, so you will see a lot of him. And of course there is Sonia Knightley the base manager, who you met earlier, if you remember? She'll be here later."

"Yes, thank you."

"Everybody," began Ernest proudly, "This is Wayland Snowball, our new clerical assistant, who will be taking over the office work from tomorrow morning." The crew laughed and smiled widely. At first Wayland thought they were laughing at his name, then he realised they were laughing at not having to do the paperwork any more. Wayland groaned inwardly.

Ernest came over and led Wayland to the large vending machine. "Now, this is Ainsley. Say hello to Wayland, Ainsley."

"Hello Wayland, how are you today?" Said a bright but sexless voice.

"I'm fine, thank you." Replied Wayland, feeling a little foolish. Talking to robots was one thing, they had eyes and mouths and shit, but this thing was just a large plastic plate.

"Can I get you anything?" Ainsley asked.

Wayland hadn't eaten all day, but he didn't have much of an appetite. "I'll just have a sandwich, if you don't mind, beef, salted, on thick white bread with real butter. And a glass of lager."

"Ok Wayland, I'll see what I can do." Ainsley hummed quietly for a minute or two, then a panel opened revealing a plate and a chipped mug. Wayland reached in and took the items. He was just about to move away, when he noticed the plate contained only a small pile of salt, and the mug had plain water in it.

"Er, I … " He began.

Ernest put his arm around Wayland's shoulder and guided him away.

"Listen, don't say anything to Ainsley, he gets upset. You see, we are a long way from H.Q. and the supply situation is a bit hit and miss. It looks like Ainsley is having problems getting ingredients, so he just gives you what he's got." Ernest pointed to Wayland's plate. "Look, you ordered beef with salt on white bread. So, no bread, no beef, no butter, but, as we can gather salt locally, you get the salt. Also, we haven't had alcohol here in months, so a mug of water is all you can expect. Looks like all the glasses have gone too. Don't worry, you'll get used to it."

Wayland wasn't really listening, the words 'No alcohol' were running around his brain, along with 'Wayland slept with Marlo,' pushing and shoving each other to get away from shutup the axeman. He went off to his room early, not bothering to find out what, if anything, Ainsley actually had in stock, as it were.

Chapter Five

In and Out

"Fuck 'em! Fuck 'em all." hissed Wayland eloquently.

Wayland was curled up on his bed like a baby. He was feeling sorry for himself, thinking how shitty the last month had been. Eating terrapins whilst drunk, crawling around an air shaft ruining his knees, having his brains numbed by stocktaking, having his knackers stomped by dykes, being shafted up the glamour-and-glitter by his so called best friend when too drunk to resist. And now he had landed up in the arse end of nowhere, at a weirdo's convention without any alcohol. And, the real possibility of being starved to death, but no way of being screwed into the same state.

Right, he thought, this is my plan of action; Avoid all dykes like the plague, as soon as possible have surgery to have my gonads put inside, get off this stinking compost heap of a planet as fast as I can, and, never get drunk with a virgin, of either sex.

This didn't really help, but what else could he do? He wasn't due for a bath until next week, and anyway he didn't know where the bathroom was. A few hours later a face appeared beside him, making him jerk with fright. Sergeant Pettybone smiled at him, "Hello son, hearing not too good? I could have killed you right there. Got to learn to keep yourself alert."

Pettybone stripped naked, much to Wayland's horror, and began doing press-ups. At one hundred and thirty seven Wayland stopped counting. Pettybone then turned over and did several hundred sit-ups. After, and still hardly even sweating, he did several other strenuous exercises, then walked out of the room with just a towel over his shoulder.

He returned exactly one minute later, showered and refreshed. Again he leaned over and spoke to Wayland, "Did you touch my books and open my wardrobe?"

"Yes, I was looking for some storage space." Wayland tried to smile, but it looked more like a grimace.

"This time, no problem, next time ask, I don't want to have to warn you again."

"Ok No problem. I'm Wayland," said Wayland nervously, trying to calm the situation, "I didn't catch your name."

"Yes you did son, It's sergeant, that's my name, not my rank, I was a captain in the special services, Psycho Killer Company, Quiet-Ones-Are-The-Worst Platoon. Motto; Who kills the most, wins."

"Oh, er, that's nice." Stuttered Wayland.

"Nice? It wasn't nice. It was blood and guts up to your armpits, it was slashing throats and ripping gizzards, it was shooting red hot lead and laser beams into soft human tissue, watching it fly apart or bubble into a steaming pile of blood and snot. Glorious, exciting, yes, but never nice." Pettybone paused, took a breath, then continued more calmly. "Look at this," He showed Wayland a lump in his forearm, about an inch across, only visible when he tightened the skin. "That's where my link was, to my power suit, like a slim suit of armour, controlled directly via the brain. Very fast, very strong. I had other attachments too, most of which were removed when I retired. Some I've still got." Sergeant turned around and pointed at his right buttock, "I've got a concealed weapon in there."

Wayland looked away quickly, thinking 'I know how you feel.' He tried to change the subject, "So, how did you end up here?"

Pettybone's eyes seemed to cloud over, a red anger that soon vanished as he controlled himself. "Well, when you've only got room for one security guy, that one has to be very good, and I am. Not to brag you understand, a man has to know what he can and can't do. I could kill you in several dozen ways. Either from many miles away or right here, quietly, without any weapons. I come from a long line of military heroes, hence the name. When I was three my dad bought me my first rabbit, then he made me sneak up on it and kill it with my wind-up train. What a guy, I was heartbroken when he died. Still, picking a fight with a gang of bouncers wasn't a good idea, especially at ninety one. But at least he died fighting, and he got inside the night club."

"And there was mother of course, a wonderful woman. She used to wrestle yaks for charity. She taught me how to gut and clean the rabbit. You know, a rabbit's fur peels right off like a pair of old pyjamas, one or two cuts around the legs, and off it pops. We all had rabbit stew that night, gathered in the kitchen in radiation suits, drinking melted snow. Happy days." Pettybone sighed fondly.

Great, thought Wayland, another one to add to the list, sharing a room with a psychopathic assassin. When will it all end? How can things possibly get worse? This last thought was a question of expectation rather than challenge, he knew something would come along.

Pettybone flexed his muscles, which bulged and tightened. "I've got such a strong grip, I'm afraid to masturbate in case I pull my dick off. So I have to get someone else to do it for me."

Wayland lay on his bunk, groaning quietly to himself.

* * * *

The next morning Wayland awoke to the sound of a blaring siren.

"Wake up kid, six thirty. Time to be up and at 'em." Yelled Pettybone, leaning over from his bunk. Wayland tucked his head under his pillow in a vain attempt to shut out the noise. After several more minutes the siren stopped. It took Wayland a while to realise it was Pettybone's alarm clock.

"Come on boy, a five mile run around the cargo holds and you'll feel great. No? Suit yourself, you may regret it one day." With that parting shot, Sergeant Pettybone disappeared out of the door. Wayland had a sudden urge to follow him, just to see if all this was just bullshit. The old guy probably just ran out of sight and sat down for a while with his finger up his arse, as Wayland's granny used to say. He decided against it, leave the old fool with some illusions. Besides it was cold out there.

Wayland had been told to report to the laboratory at nine a.m. So, starting has he meant to go on, he got up at eight fifty, got dressed, had a piss and a drink of water and went to work. He followed the cerise line, emerging in a converted hanger. The whole space was filled with lab equipment and plants. Large tubs stood beside benches filled with apparatus which fed pipes and wires into the soil. Steamy greenhouses stood along the walls, with silhouetted leafy shapes and flashing lights within. Along the ceiling the vines he had seen outside clung to the metal girders. Wayland walked further in, looking for signs of human life.

One of the vines dropped down and coiled itself around him several times, like a thick, green snake, then began to squeeze. "Hello, er, I'm here." he said hoarsely. Not a sound of human activity, not even a whisper, just the clicking of some machine somewhere. The vine, sensing fear, began to raise itself up, pulling Wayland onto his tip-toes. It was just about to shake the shit out of him when a voice sounded behind him.

"Morning Wayland, you're keen. When we said nine o'clock, we meant nine fifteen-nine thirtyish. But no matter, you're here now. The guy at Headquarters said you were something a bit different. I see you've met Sarah, our watch vine. She won't let strangers in here without a fight." Ernest walked passed grinning. "If you'll come over here I'll tell you where your desk is."

The vine, sensing that it wasn't allowed to strangle this soft thing, gave one last pinch then let Wayland go. He watched it pull back up to the ceiling with relief, promising to bring a flame thrower tomorrow. Wayland made his way through the tangle of natural and artificial growths until he found a small office. It was almost completely obscured, but luckily not filled like the rest of the room. Stepping in, he may have been walking into any normal office, complete with filing cabinets, computers and telephones. Ernest was sitting in a swivel chair writing on an old-fashioned note pad.

"These are your duties and responsibilities for today, and probably most days, too. It's all the usual office stuff, which you are familiar with, plus the gathering of the monitor printouts and readings disks, which are fed into the computer." He turned and grinned at Wayland. "Ok Any problems? No, good. I'll see you later." He strode from the room.

Wayland looked swiftly around the office, "Is it all right to put the kettle on?" He shouted after Ernest's back.

"If you really want to, but don't burn your head." Answered Ernest. Wayland shook his head, "What a prat, I think he's serious."

"Talking to yourself, young man?" Doctor Crippen appeared round the office door. "I know a cure for that." She advanced across the floor towards him. Wayland backed off, trying to put something solid between them, like a planet, but a desk was all he could find. Dr Crippen stopped suddenly and said, "Did you mention a kettle, I'd love a cup of tea." She smiled primly. Lionel ambled slowly into the room, "Bloody hell, he's keen, look at the time, and he's making tea." He yawned.

Wayland had no choice now but to make tea for everyone, including Sean, who turned up several minutes later looking like he was still asleep. Wayland hadn't meant to start this habit, making drinks for everyone, you ended up making them all the time. So, he put two tea bags in each cup, left them in for five minutes, then stirred it with an old tooth brush he found in a draw. He added one tablespoon of sugar to each cup then took them out on a tray. Everyone agreed this was the best tea they had ever tasted, strong and sweet, just the thing to get you going in the morning. The Doctor had winked at him when she said the last bit. Then they all said he could make tea like this every day.

Just before lunch the intercom from the landing pad crackled into life. "Delivery for you, supplies and shit, I'll leave it here." Said a strange, nervous, let's-get-out-of-here kind of voice. Sean and Lionel came rushing into the office,

"Wayland, quick get up there before the vines take the stuff, those yellow bastards do this every time." Lionel cursed. Sean agreed with a shake of his afro.

Wayland sprinted from the office, through the lab, watching carefully for Sarah. He had gone some distance when he realised he couldn't remember which line led to the landing pad. He had come in that way not long ago, but he was paying more attention to Ernest than where he was going. He suddenly remembered it was a blue line, like a blue film, but there wasn't a blue line here. Then he noticed the red line, which he knew led to the infirmary then the blue line from there.

He pelted off, running as fast as he could. Twenty feet later he slowed to a walk, a burning stitch in his side. Well, he thought, I did my best, I'm a C.A. not a bloody security guard. Several minutes later, after following the red line the wrong way, he found the infirmary and the blue line. Following this brought him at last to the landing pad door.

The door hissed open as he turned the handle. A thick cloud of moisture, smelling of salad, hit him in the face as he stepped out. It was hot out here today, humid and sticky, he could almost hear the plants growing. Wayland climbed the metal steps, through the retreating vines, rather nervously, and onto the platform. Several small, and one large box sat to one side of the landing pad. The vines were already examining the parcels, even pulling some of the smaller ones away. "Hey! Get out of there." He shouted, then felt rather silly. But to his surprise the vines pulled back, dropping the boxes they had been fondling.

He managed to pull the smaller ones inside fairly quickly, but the larger one took some effort. It was about as big as a small fridge, but a lot heavier. The steps were giving him a problem, how to get this big thing down there? If it's this heavy it should be safe until I can get help, he thought. Walking down the steps, he searched out the intercom on the door. "Er, I need a hand with this big one, anybody, please." He said hesitantly. He sat on the floor inside to wait.

Half an hour later, Sean turned up with a trolley. "This might help." He smiled that bright smile again, then returned to looking bored. Wayland rose from the floor, then turned towards the steps. "It's just this heavy one … " The box was at the bottom of the steps, intact, not a mark on it. Sean experimentally pushed on the box. "Wow, man, how'd you get that down the steps? You're stronger than you look." He smiled for quite sometime. Wayland looked around suspiciously, at the vines, at the surrounding vegetation, but there was no one around.

Together, they loaded up the large box, then the smaller ones on top. With Wayland pushing, and Sean pulling they soon had the supplies in the storage area. Everyone, even Sonia, was waiting for them when they got there. It seemed it was a memorable day when the stores finally turned up. Sonia held a clipboard to which was attached a long list. "Right, you shout out what's turned up, I'll try and match it to what was ordered."

She turned to Wayland. "We have this every time we order anything. They seem to send a random selection of goods, no matter what we send for. For instance, we haven't ordered anything as big or heavy as that box." She pointed with her chewed pencil at the big crate. "Let's all open something small, and compare." There was an air of excited tension as everyone picked a likely looking box and began to open it.

Wayland picked up a square box about as big as his head. He prised the lid back and opened an inner sealed bag. "Shout it out Wayland, don't be shy." Sonia chirped up.

"Sntytlls." mumbled Wayland.

"Sorry? Didn't get that."

"Sanitary towels," He said a little louder. Great, he thought just my luck, women's things.

"Oh, good, I've been waiting for those. I ordered those … " she consulted her list. "Here it is … eleven months ago. That's not bad."

Several others called out items, most of which were food or lab supplies, ordered from between six months and two years previously. No wonder they didn't rush to work, there was probably nothing to do. "Right, let's go for the big one. Let's see, we haven't yet accounted for … winter blankets from last spring, Christmas puddings from the Christmas before last … and one hundred millilitre self-propelled pipettes.

Sean and Lionel set about the box with small crow bars. The lid splintered and cracked before finally coming loose. The rest of the crowd gathered around silently, some wishing for the blankets, others on the side of Christmas puddings. Lionel lifted the lid clear and peered in, "No, it's a photocopier." There were groans all around. The crowd began to pack the supplies away, taking any they needed for themselves.

"Hey!" Shouted Ernest, "look what I found in the grocery box, extra thick chunky-chilli relish." He held up the jar in triumph. Everyone smiled or cheered. No one noticed Wayland discreetly covering his genital region with both hands.

In the next few weeks, Wayland settled into a fairly boring routine of tea making and entering results into various recording devices. He never fully understood what the scientists were measuring, or why, but it made him feel important to be involved. He was sitting in the office trying to look busy whilst thinking about Sonia tied upright to a wardrobe by her silk knickers. He had been fantasising more and more about what he saw as the only available totty. Despite his best efforts and real strong come-on, she had so far resisted his charm and kept her knees pressed tightly together.

Wayland sometimes wondered if someone else was giving her one, but he never saw her alone with any of the others. Perhaps she was frigid like most of the woman on this planet. Must be something in the water. Lionel walked in shaking his head, bursting the thought bubble in Wayland's.

"How can I get proper CO_2 readings with this thing?" He wafted a pen like instrument with a blunt tip in Wayland's face.

"Why don't you order a new one, from the main base?" Asked Wayland.

"You've seen what happens, who knows what they'll send if I order one of these. Plastic explosives, fridge magnets, lime douches? I'll just have to tape this back together." Lionel stalked out with a roll of plastic tape.

Later that day, Wayland asked Sonia about their ordering problems. It was a great chat up line, full of smutty innuendo, but Sonia remained maddeningly calm. Will of iron that woman, thought Wayland, then giggled at the image it conjured.

"So," he said nonchalantly, "you aren't getting enough on a regular basis, supplies and sh … stuff?"

"No, it's very frustrating sometimes. Look, I'll show you." Sonia pulled up a form on the computer screen. "This is a standard ordering form, item name, amount, other details, and part number." She tapped the monitor screen, "We don't have part number listings, when we ask they say the numbers are listed in the part numbers catalogue, if we would like to order one. But they won't tell us the part number of the catalogue. When we ask for the part number they say it's on the front cover of the catalogue." She grimaced. "We just can't win. So, we make do as best we can." She leaned closer to Wayland, her left breast practically touching his shoulder. Mr Stiffy woke up.

"Do you know what I haven't had for ages?" Her breath was warm on Wayland's ear. Yes! He wanted to say, a damn good seeing to. Mr Stiffy began to expand. "No, what?" He whispered hoarsely.

"Ice cream. What I would do for one mouthful of chocolate chip and almond ice cream." She groaned, a deep, throaty, sensuous moan. Mr Stiffy began to pulse. She straightened and headed for the office door, "Oh well, can't have everything." She sighed as she walked out. Mr Stiffy wouldn't go away. Damn, thought Wayland, another trip to the toilet with the rubber gloves and the baby oil.

In the deepest, darkest recesses of Wayland's mind, where the blood never flows and synapses go around in threes, a tiny idea came into being. When it didn't immediately get jumped by gangs of alcohol molecules out for a good time, or get stamped on by large accretions of neglect, it started to grow. Once it had reached a large enough size, it began to fight its way through the forest of pre-conception and up the hill of bigotry, towards the dim light that was Wayland's conscious mind. Several hours later it emerged triumphant, to find Wayland asleep.

The idea looked across the plain of sickness that was Wayland's dreamscape. A woman, dressed in see-through leather and fluffy bunny slippers was being chased across the plain by a large wardrobe. The item of furniture had a large erection in the shape of a coat-hanger. The idea sat down, closed its eyes, and waited patiently for morning.

Wayland had come to ignore Sergeant's alarm clock, whilst Sergeant had given up trying to wake Wayland. Most mornings he was allowed to wake up slowly, which was how he liked it. This particular morning he had woken with a flaming hard-on and a thought niggling at the back of his mind. He tried to remember his dream, but it had already gone. The thought, though still there, proved elusive.

He staggered out of bed and began to dress. One of his shoes was missing, forcing him to get down on all fours and look for it. As he looked under the bed a large wedge of paper caught his eye. The idea woke suddenly and began jumping up and down shouting. Wayland moved the paper to one side to look for his shoe. The idea ran around, thumped its fists against the ground, did all it could to grab his attention.

Wayland found the shoe and put it on. Then, checking his flies for the last time, he headed for the door. The small idea pulled out a long knife and hurled it with all its might at the small glowing light. Wayland stopped with his hand on the door handle. He stood still for a moment, then retraced his steps. He pulled the paper from under the bed. It was the listing he had been given for his stint in the warehouse. Wayland looked hopefully at the top page. Sure enough, there it was; column heading, "Part Numbers."

Wayland was as happy as he had been for some time, he was about to rush off and tell everyone, then he thought, no, he would surprise them.

The small idea, its task completed, died.

When he skipped into the lab, a huge grin on his face, he found it full of noise and movement. "What's going on?" He asked the first person he saw, who happened to be Sean. His face brightening smile flashed on, "Field trip man." Sean beamed, then dashed away. Making his way to the office, Wayland asked everyone he passed what a field trip was. Finally, Dr Crippen explained, "You know, a tour, a trip into the wilds to find new plants." She pointed towards a leaf covered porthole, "We are going out there."

"What, everyone?" He gulped.

"Yes, even you," answered Sonia.

Wayland's face turned a deathly pale, "Oh, shit!" He squeaked.

Chapter Six

Down, Down and away

"Two weeks!"

"Oh yes, it takes time to plan these things you know. You can't just rush off into that jungle without proper planning."

Wayland sighed with relief, he had thought they were going today. On the other hand it gave him time to think up really horrible things that could happen to him, and dream about them too.

"Besides, we may be able to get a few items we need if we order them today. I don't suppose we'll get everything, but it's worth a try." Said Sonia.

"I can do the ordering if you like, I know what to do, if you just make a list and I'll get on with it." Said Wayland casually.

"Yes, that would be great. You know, I'll bet your manager is regretting the day he let you go." She smiled.

Sonia had the team draw up a list of supplies, and things they needed anyway. During his lunch hour, Wayland dashed back to their room. Luckily Pettybone was always on patrol somewhere at this time of the day. Hastily he looked through the list, matching the items described as nearly as he could with the printed list. Then he copied the part numbers onto a separate piece of paper, making doubly sure he had the number for chocolate chip and almond ice cream.

When the office was quiet, in the middle of the afternoon, Wayland entered the numbers into the computer and transmitted the order. Feeling very pleased with himself, he leaned back in his chair and daydreamed for the rest of the day.

* * * *

Almost two weeks later, and the day before their scheduled departure, a shuttle made the usual hit and run delivery. Sean O'Meara helped Wayland with the load, the usual bored look on his dark face. Wayland tried not to smile, wait until you see this lot man, your face will light up the whole building.

They were crowded into the storage area, as before, waiting for the delivery. They were all smiling, but not very hopeful. The pile of items was unusually big this time, someone commented. They've probably sent three of everything like they did before, someone else answered. Wayland was very tense waiting for the first package to be opened.

"Hey, I actually ordered one of these!" Exclaimed Lionel, holding a pen-like object up for everyone to see. A small smile appeared on his face. When the next three items also matched what had been ordered, the conversation began to get louder, matched only by the width of Wayland's smirk.

Sonia screamed, the room fell silent, "Ice cream! Look everybody, ice cream, chocolate chip and almond." She began to read the packet, "Instant ice cream, just add boiling water for that authentic Italian flavour." She turned to Wayland, a wide smile on her lips. "Thank you Wayland, I know it's not real ice cream, but that was very thoughtful of you. I don't know how you did it, but I am glad you did." She walked over to him and kissed him firmly on the cheek. He blushed like a teenage virgin caught naked in the showers by a rugby team.

"I don't believe it," Lionel laughed, "almost everything we ordered has arrived. Some twat has sent ribbed condoms instead of rigid cartons, but hell, the rest is spot on. There's actually some alcohol here." He said in amazement. Wayland was glad he was already blushing, Lionel's hand writing was terrible.

"I think we should all get this lot stowed away, then go up to the canteen to celebrate." Sonia declared. No one disagreed.

In the canteen later, Sonia proposed a toast. "To Wayland, for making our lives that bit easier." Everybody raised their assorted mugs, cups, and bottles. "To Wayland!" They all chorused, and grinned broadly. Wayland cringed in a corner, knocking back cheap lager and trying unsuccessfully not to redden.

"Now for some more good news," announced Sonia, "because of the recent intake of decent supplies we are now able to go on a longer field trip, right out to the Mammary plains."

The scientists in the team cheered loudly, obviously they had been waiting for the chance to go. Sonia turned to Wayland. "Mammary plains is an area several hundred kilometres from here. There's this long flat plain, covered with vegetation of course, and in the middle are several hundred low, rounded hills covering ten thousand square kilometres. Nobody knows how they got there, or how they were formed, but they look like a sea of breasts, hence the name. It's a place that has never been explored by humans, pure, unspoiled jungle. Who knows what we'll find out there. Isn't it exciting?" Sonia beamed at Wayland. He forced a smile, whilst thinking, 'great just bloody wonderful, out in the middle of nowhere with a bunch of weirdos and killer nipple-eating fungus behind every tree. I thought life was full of ups and downs? Mine's full of levels and downs, what happened to my ups?'

"As you all know, we can't land a shuttle there, so we will have to hike in, everybody break out your tents."

Wayland groaned, saw Sonia looking and turned it to a yawn. She walked over to him.

"You know, I was a bit dubious when your request for transfer hit my desk, I thought someone was pulling a stunt on me. But you know, you've proved to be a very valuable addition to the team. I think I might just give your ex-manager a call, tell him how well you've turned out." She squeezed his shoulder warmly, sensually, then walked away.

Wayland watched her backside as she went, mixed thoughts in his head. He would love to see Hardstaff's face, when she called, he'd think she'd gone crazy. But he would also love to be underneath her, whilst, phone in hand, she rode him like a wild stallion. Then, Mr bone came to visit, making Wayland spend longer in the toilet than was strictly necessary.

That morning everyone was up early, even Wayland got up before eight. Preparations were proceeding apace when he reached the lab. Most of the packing had been done in a feverish, late-night session. Sean had been smiling constantly for almost an hour, his bright smile spreading to all the rest. Even Sergeant Pettybone smiled, very slightly, but still a smile.

They had decided to meet in one of the old hangers. The cargo bay doors had been jacked open, revealing a curtain of climbers. Lionel and Ernest had set too and tied them back like posh drapes, leaving a large hole in the middle. Sonia appeared, ubiquitous clipboard in hand, mounted a small crate and waited for everyone's attention. "Right, listen up everybody. We'll stick to the plan we had prepared before. Wayland, I'll fill you in on the details later. Meanwhile, it's down to the river for rendezvous with the shuttle. Sergeant, if you would like to take the robots first, to clear a path."

Sergeant clicked to attention, "Yes ma'am. Unit one, take point, unit two, follow five metres behind. At the double!"

Two square boxes, like fridges on tracks, trundled out of a packing case and headed for the door. They were featureless, black lumps that creaked slightly when they moved. The two units moved through the plants, crushing everything in their way.

"Delicate little buggers, aren't they?" whispered Lionel. "Sergeant loves them, some say literally. But rules is rules, and rules say we have to have at least two drones with defensive weaponry on all trips into the bush. Not gonna find a lot with those brutes squashing it all."

"They've got guns and things, like live ammo?" queried Wayland nervously.

"Oh yes. All sorts of stuff. Originally anti-alien robots. Every kind of weapon for the destruction, disablement and capture of organic life-forms, in that order. Ask Sean, he re-programmed them when they arrived, he can tell you what's inside, although he let Sergeant resume responsibility for them later. I think he was trying to stop him getting bored, but old Pettybone took a real shine to them." Lionel smiled, picked up his rucksack and joined the procession.

The cargo bay doors bonged ominously shut behind them after the last person out. Sergeant did something with a small black box, a light began to flash at the side of the door. "That should keep people out." He grinned then stalked back to the front of the column. Wayland looked around, trying to find the hoards of cat-burglars and ram-raiders hiding behind the trees. He tutted loudly, shaking his head, "weird, very weird." He breathed.

Three hours and one hairy, low level flight later, they we off-loaded onto a sandbank beside the river, rather too rapidly for Wayland's liking. The shuttle sped off, promising to return when called for. The robots were already on their way into the jungle by the time Wayland was loaded up and ready. Shutup the axeman still had two thoughts to chase, 'no alcohol' had been caught and chopped to bits after the short drinking session, but had been replaced with 'I hate plants'.

The sandbank was made up of strange cubic grains of pale green sand which crinkled musically when trod on. Wayland walked around for a few minutes trying to play a tune. His eye was drawn to a propeller shaped flower rising from a low bush at the edge of the water. Whilst the rest of the group checked their kit and formed up into a line, Wayland went to investigate. He was strangely attracted to the red flower by a rather pungent mix of odours. Getting close up he could pick out the individual scents of beer, pizza dough and sweaty fannies. Wayland was hooked, he leaned over to inhale a good nose full. Unsurprisingly, the flower lurched suddenly upwards, planting its petals firmly against his left cheek.

For the several seconds it took for the signal to batter

its way to Wayland's skull, he stood still, feeling slightly foolish, with a red flower attached to his face. Then he roared in pain, a deep throaty panic-driven scream that would have done the cheapest of horror films proud.

The other members of the party froze for a few moments, then came rushing in syncopation across the sand. Sean, with his long legs, reached him first. He grabbed the flower and ripped it off, leaving a red wheal on Wayland's face. Dr Crippen elbowed her way to the front and grabbed Wayland's chin, turning his face this way and that. She brought her face closer, at first Wayland thought she was going to kiss him. His stomach turned.

"Yes, there's definitely something in there, some kind of seed." Said Enid, "I'll have to operate." Wayland went extremely pale. Noticing his lack of colour, Enid reassured him. "It's all right young man, I didn't mean operate in that sense, the seed has got to come out, but I think my tweezers will do the job." She smiled reassuringly.

Everyone gathered around to watch, a circle of faces peering at him. The tweezers were expertly wielded, and soon the long, flat seed had been extracted. The scientists gathered noisily around the container in which the doctor had dropped the seed, muttering comments and questions. Only the doctor remained. "That's quite a mark on your face I'm afraid, looks like a burn, probably some kind of acid in the flower. You may have to face the fact of extensive plastic surgery, or a life times disfigurement. I'll dress it lightly for now, come and see me later, for some painkillers if you need them. Dr Crippen joined the others around the bush.

Sean and Lionel had pulled out long-handled pruners, clipping bits off the bush and stuffing them into sample jars. All the while excitedly chattering about new discoveries and fame and fortune. Wayland stood quietly as the group packed up again and moved off into the jungle. Great, thought Wayland, just as people were starting to like me a sodding plant gives me the kiss of ugly and I'm scarred for life. What next, what fucking next?

He followed the group, who in turn followed the environmentally hostile robots, for what seemed like months. Eventually, Sonia called a halt. They had a brief lunch from their packs, then carried on. The whole group were unusually quiet as they moved, Wayland especially. He was keeping a tally in his head of why? questions. Why were they walking? Why am I at the back? Why can't we stop now? Why do we have to sleep in tents? Why are we going anyway? Why are we being followed by something big making a snorting noise?

The importance of the last question suddenly sank in, Wayland turned around, but saw nothing. The snorting noise stopped, only to start again as he walked on. Sonia, whose bottom Wayland had been following, noticed his behaviour and waited for him. "What's the matter Wayland?" She sounded genuinely concerned.

"Er, I think there's something following us."

Sonia looked at Wayland, then burst out laughing, "Wayland, you're so funny, you had me going then, you know as well as me that no predator bigger than a dog has ever been found on Greenshy. Now come on." She gave him a huge smile, then walked back to the rapidly disappearing column. Wayland caught up, hissing "There are some pretty big dogs, I've seen them, massive rottweilers that can rip your arms off, even while sitting in a car." Sonia laughed again, a bright sound that made Wayland smile.

He passed the rest of the time making up double entendres for Sonia, he was definitely in there if he played his cards right. 'Shall we penetrate the jungle.' 'This bush is very thick.' 'Look at those nuts.' And so on, ad nauseam.

That night they set up camp in a small clearing under a very large tree. The tents turned out to be more like hammocks, long tubes that attached to a tree at either end. A rope was tied around the large tree to anchor the ends for the whole party, the other ends were tied to a variety of trees the right distance away. Dr Crippen and Lionel tied their two tents together on one side, the rest radiated outwards like a star around the rest of the trunk. Wayland noticed with some delight that Sonia's tent was very close to his.

After a warm meal and a few hushed conversations, the group began to drift off to bed. Lionel and Enid went first, clutching each other's bums. He heard Lionel say, "I've never done it in a hammock." Wayland cringed, how disgusting, pumping up and down on an old woman!

Sergeant placed the two drones either side of the camp, giving them orders to guard it at all costs. The backs of the robots opened, revealing short, but wide gun barrels. Wayland was in two minds about this, ok so they can blast anything nasty to a pulp, but what if they decide we are nasty? Slowly he got up and approached his tent, moving cautiously. The robots completely ignored him.

He unzipped the tent and rolled in, sealing it again straight away. He was surprised to find the thing bigger than he had thought. It even had a light inside, which of course he immediately switched on. Apparently, it was fully attuned to his needs, letting in enough air to keep him at a constant temperature, but keeping out unwanted wildlife, at least that's what it said on a flap inside. There was just enough room to get undressed, although it swung alarmingly. Wayland crawled into the sleeping bag and settled down.

Gently, he traced the scar on his face, it didn't really hurt now, just tingled slightly. The flower had left its mark of three petals right in the middle of his cheek. It could have been worse he supposed, he had seen some really ugly scars. Marlo had told him that some women found them attractive, gave the man a worldly, well travelled look. But Marlo was a virgin, with women at least, so what did he know?

A strange thrumming noise started to rattle the anchor rope. Wayland wondered if the tree was going to move in the night, dragging them all screaming into the darkness. Then he heard low moaning sounds and realised it was only Lionel and Enid bonking.

He was awakened some time later by a breath of cool air and a strange noise. He suddenly realised the noise was the zip being pulled back. Oh no, he thought I'm too young to die, eaten alive by a zip-undoing alien. A head popped through the hole, Sonia smiled shyly at him. "Well, aren't you going to invite me in? It's cold out here."

"Er, yes of course, er, squeeze in." he made room for her beside him. As she rolled in he realised she was stark naked apart from a pair of stout boots, which dropped to the ground as she pulled her legs up. She undid the sleeping bag and slid in next to him. Mr bone shot up like a self-inflating life raft.

"So, what now, boss?" Wayland said quietly.

"Get those pants off and show me a good time. That's an order." She smiled. Wayland hesitated, which puzzled Sonia. She looked at him, then at the scar, "It doesn't bother me Way, it isn't that big, besides it looks more like a tattoo. Honest, there isn't a problem on this side of the fence." She wrapped her arms around Wayland's neck and pulled him against her.

Wayland kissed her on the lips then went straight for her tits, one hand on the right, his lips around the left. He began to suck the nipple then kissed across her chest and up to her other …

Wayland froze, there was no other nipple! He didn't know what to do, he had never done this sort of thing before. Shall I make my way back to the other nipple and pretend I haven't noticed? Perhaps it fell off in the dark and … no, get a grip. Wayland started to move his mouth back to her left breast, but too late, Sonia had noticed his hesitation. "You don't like me now do you?" She said tearfully. "Just because I've only got one nipple, I'm not a whole woman." A tear ran down her face towards her ear.

"No, it's alright, it's just a bit of a surprise. It doesn't matter, this one is very nice." Wayland said tenderly, which surprised the hell out of him. He carried on kissing and touching her until she stopped crying and started moaning. He was put off by the missing nipple, his eyes were constantly drawn to where it should be. But Mr bone was ready and willing, 'I don't care if she's got one nipple or four, if she's got a twat, I'm going to fuck it.' He kept on insisting.

Several minutes of belly-bashing later, Sonia suddenly tensed and started groaning. At first Wayland thought she was having a fit and was just about to ram a piece of wood between her teeth, like he'd seen in films. He realised with surprise and a certain amount of pride that she was actually having an orgasm! Well, that's a first, he thought, things are looking up.

Lying together after, Sonia complimented him on his technique, "I haven't had such good sex in years. You showed a lot of control to say you can't have had any for a few months at least." She looked up at him with moist brown eyes.

"Yes, it must be that long, but, you know, ladies first and all that." Wayland managed to sound almost sincere, but it was the battle he had been fighting with his dick that had kept him going, almost to double figures. His high brain had been saying, "No, she's deformed, get away." which had cooled his passion. His low brain had shouted, "No, this might be your only chance, go for it!" In the end of course the jelly effect had won hands down.

Looking closely now he had the time, he noticed her nipple, not missing, no scar or marks, just not there, like it never had been. "What ... where did, you know." he gesture vaguely over her chest.

"What? Oh that. You may have heard rumours about nipple-eating fungus?" Wayland nodded. "Well, it wasn't a fungus, more like a virus, but with selective feeding habits. It didn't so much eat as convert, taking the proteins and stripping off what it needed. The waste products it replaced where it found them, with bits missing of course. Hence this." She grabbed her tit and pointed the rounded end at Wayland. It was remarkable, the way the structure had been preserved. Another first, to look at a woman's breast without wanting to rub a part of his anatomy against it.

"So, the lab people studied it, couldn't find a cure, but found a substance it didn't like, sort of drove it out. The doctors say I can have surgery if I want. A reshape and a sort of tattoo. I was thinking about going for it on my next leave. What do you think?"

Momentarily, Wayland was stunned, someone asking him what he thought, then waiting for an answer was very rare in his life.

"Oh, I think you should, you know, just for your own self-esteem."

"You're very perceptive, Wayland, not like other men I've known. I think you're going to go far." Sonia sat up and smiled, "I'd better get back, we don't want people accusing me of favouritism. See you later." She bent and kissed him warmly then slipped out of the tent. A whispered cursing could be heard as she tried to find her boots in the dark, then all went quiet.

Wayland laid back, hands behind his head, so, she thinks I'm perceptive, he thought, smiling widely. As soon as we get back I'm going to find out what it means.

The next morning, although Sonia was all smiles, she didn't particularly favour Wayland. They broke camp and marched off in the same order as yesterday; robot one, Sergeant, robot two, Ernest, Lionel, Enid, Sean, Sonia and Wayland. Several times, when no one else was watching, Sonia turned around and smiled lasciviously at him. Wayland wondered, with some apprehension, if this was leading into a relationship. He gulped, forced a smile and carried on walking, looking at all the fascinating greenery around him.

Chapter Seven

The Hard Way

"Mammaries ahoy!" Lionel shouted in the late afternoon of the third day. They had travelled without incident, and any further tent-swinging, deep into the jungle. The densely packed trees prevented them seeing the hills until the trail turned suddenly upwards. The robots had informed them that they were on course, meter by meter, thanks to their satellite positioning equipment. But still it was satisfying to see the first hills for themselves.

The first night they camped half way up the first hill. An early supper was followed by a noisy discussion on plans and tactics. Most of the talk went over Wayland's head, words like 'quartering search patterns' and 'parallel evolution' meant nothing to him. So he just sat quietly, wondering what Sonia would taste like when he first went down on her.

With all the details settled, and the teams decided, he noticed he was in Sonia's team with Lionel and Enid, they all went to bed, ready for an early start.

* * * *

Wayland was surprised at the uniformity of the hills, or rather he thought they all looked the same. They had been wandering around a randomly chosen hill in circles at different heights, giving him plenty of opportunity to look around. Enid explained they were examining the cross section of plants at different altitudes and different aspects. She then, noticing his blank look, explained about height and the position of the sun.

His job was mainly to carry or hold various sticks,

squares and measuring instruments. They were all surprisingly light and no trouble at all to carry, so he didn't really mind. One of the instruments, a small pen-like thing, was used for measuring distance. He particularly liked this one because it shot a thin laser light out of one end. Somehow, Wayland didn't understand how, the pen then told you the distance from you to the thing you aimed at. "Four metres twenty," he would say. Spinning around he would shoot something else, "Aha, eight metres forty five.". The others put up with this for sometime before Enid gave him a sharp look. From then on he kept his measuring to himself.

Sonia visited his tent on a couple of occasions, he went to hers once, but the threatened relationship didn't really develop. Sonia was busy with her work and Wayland was trying to be cool. They still screwed with some vigour, those few times, but Wayland felt she was holding back, they rarely even touched except in bed. When Enid and Lionel were out of sight around the hill, Sonia was still very distant. Wayland decided she was using him for sex, so if that was all she wanted, fine. But secretly he was a little upset. Women! He complained quietly.

After a few days of hill circling, the teams decided to move further into the range, to look for different habitats. The line formed up again and off they went. A long walk followed, with no one explaining to him why. Wayland began to sulk. He lagged behind the rest, always keeping Sonia just in sight. The tracks made by the robots were easy enough to follow, but it made sense to be doubly sure. Unfortunately, Wayland didn't have any, so soon lost sight of the group. He followed the tracks, not feeling particularly concerned.

About an hour later he noticed the tracks split up, one lot going right around a hill, the others going left along a valley. Oh great! He thought, nobody told me they were splitting up, and which one is my team? Hill or valley, he thought. Valley, I've always preferred valleys. It didn't really matter, although there were no women in the other team. Still, it wasn't forever, They could always send him back.

Another few hours later, and no sign of anyone, Wayland stopped. He sank down to the ground with his back against a tree, pulling out his water bottle. The water was still cold in the special flask, it refreshed him, but made him hungry. He sat for a while, looking up and down the trail. Examining the tracks, he noticed how clever it was for them to pass either side of the great tree trunks. Wayland had rested, got up and walked for almost an hour before the thought reached the murky depths of his logic centre. Eyes wide, he turned, looked at the tracks going either side of trees and bushes. He ran back along the trail, noticed the tracks draw together to pass between two large trees, then widen out again. Turning on one foot, he leapt along the tracks, towards whatever was making them.

The tracks continued for some distance up the hill. Wayland was sweating and out of breath when he reached the point where the tracks disappeared, down a small hole. Wayland put his hands to his head and screamed in rage and fear. Lost! Lost and alone in a god-forsaken shit pile! Led into a trap by who knows what, to starve slowly to death on a giant grow-bag of a planet, bursting with life and nothing to eat.

It had started to grow dark when Wayland suddenly realised he could follow the tracks back to where they split. Quickly he ran along the tracks in the increasing gloom, fear lending speed to his wary, out of condition, let's face it, blubbery, frame. While the light lasted he re-traced his steps, until at last he flopped down on a loop of sensor vine, too exhausted to move. The light faded out, leaving him in almost total darkness. For a man of his generation, darkness was almost unknown. With cheap power and high technology almost everything had a light of one form or another, even the dildo he had found under his mum's bed once, or had that been a torch?

Realising he did have a light, the laser measurer, he sat upright and fumbled in his pocket. He withdrew the small cylinder and switched it on. A bright, but very tiny light illuminated a small area exactly two metres twelve away. Damn, he thought, about as much use as a waterproof teabag.

Wayland felt around in the dark. The vine was hung in hoops behind him. He climbed up a few of them and settled at two metres sixty above the ground. Sonia and Enid had explained to him about the lack of wildlife on the planet. Yes it was bursting with plant life of many kinds, but animals were comparatively rare. No one knew why yet, but it was suspected the planet was either very young or very old, the animals had either not evolved yet or had somehow gone extinct. It seemed the plants filled most of the evolution niches anyway, with the sensor vines being dominant.

Which meant, in practical terms, that no stonking great nightmare of a thing was going to rip him open from throat to knackers then eat his entrails. Wayland climbed a bit higher, not liking the last thought at all. Four metres, that should do it.

With great effort, and the imagining of several very specialised sex acts, he managed to stay awake for a couple of hours. Finally, nestling into a loop of vine, he fell asleep. He dreamed that giant snakes had come alive from the trees, dropping down on him as he slept, entangling him in their furry arms. Waking with a start, he looked around, forgetting where he was.

It was sometime after dawn, the sun not yet fully up. The vines around him formed an angled hammock, supporting him in all the right places. That was lucky, finding a spot that just fitted me, he thought. Carefully he climbed down to the jungle floor, looking around for the tracks. A heavy dew lay on the ground, causing the leaf litter to swell and slide. Of the tracks there was no sign, either one way or the other.

Wayland did what most city boys would do in this situation, he sat down and waited for help.

Neither a passing tourist in a mobile home, nor a curious village bobby passed by. The R.A.C. were noticeable by their absence, and the friendly German backpacker and his Swedish wife never put in an appearance. It finally sunk in to Wayland's head, he would have to help himself. So, he drank the rest of his water, as there didn't seem to be anything else for breakfast, then went on his way.

Re-tracing his steps around the first hill was easy, he had walked with his right hand up hill, so he walked with his left hand up hill until he came to a valley. He was fairly certain he had come down this valley, but he hadn't been paying that much attention. Well, he thought, they must be looking for me now, I'll follow this route until they find me.

Several hours later he still hadn't been rescued. Wayland was starting to lose patience, if they didn't get here soon he was going to have to spend another night in the trees. Also, there was nothing to eat around here. His throat was drying quickly in the hot atmosphere, and it had been several years since he had taken any major exercise. In fact the last time he'd been out of breath was on top of Olivia Dumphy, but he had brewers droop then, and was fighting a loosing battle. And she was so pissed she thought he was Rod and Bob Noblett, the twins from upstairs.

A likely looking valley opened up between two hills on his right. It led straight for quite a way. Ah! This is it, he thought, wrongly as it went, but he had a lot of confidence in his decision. Boldly, he started along it, beginning to admire the view as he went. If you looked close enough, it wasn't just green, there were all different shades, from light green to dark green, and various flowers and fruits, and bracts. That was a word Sonia had taught him 'bracts'. He quite liked the sound of it, bracts. They were those coloured leaves around the flower, the ones people thought were petals, uh! Didn't they know anything?

That night Wayland slept five metres fifty nine above the ground, again on several loops of vine, which were the only plant he trusted. There were several yellow bracts nearby, which made him choose this particular spot. Sentimental old fool, he thought. By now his mouth was very dry, his stomach thought his throat had healed up, and Mr Stiffy had gone into hibernation. Tomorrow, he vowed, I must find food and water, even if I have to eat some fruit.

On the morning of the fourth day he had woke early. He was still lost, and still hadn't found any food or water. Again, he had picked a spot that exactly matched his body shape. "Wonderful things these sensor vines, I think I'll take one home with me," he said. As he awoke he was sure he had felt movement in the vines. A few minutes later the vines moved again, pulling their coils up from the ground. Wayland looked down to see what all the fuss was about. A strange looking animal was sitting on the bottom loop taking bites out of the vine leaves. It was the size and general shape of a large tortoise, with a knife-edged ridge along its back. This one was a light pink colour, with brown blotches in lines down its shell. A small head like a praying mantis moved back and forth while it ate.

Wayland's first thought was 'breakfast', then he remembered the terrapin affair. His empty stomach jumped and lurched, food, it yelled, yes, but not that. He noticed the vine was getting very agitated, well, for a plant. So he climbed down low enough to swing his leg, and gave it a good kick.

His foot crunched into the beast with a hearty thud, the vine swung, his toe began to throb, the beast never even flinched. Wayland tried again, this time with the heel of his boot. The vine swung further, the beast withdrew its head, then carried on eating. "Right, you little munching bastard," Wayland yelled, "I'll teach you a lesson." He leaped to the ground, grabbed hold of the vine and gave it a damn good shake.

The beast stopped eating for a few moments, looked around with large, purple eyes, then carried on eating. "This is ridiculous, how can that strange looking thing stay on there?" Asked Wayland. Wayland didn't answer, merely scratched at his nuts. He bent down and looked underneath the tortoise beetle, as he had just named it. Wayland groaned, "well no wonder you couldn't shift it, look at all those legs." The entire bottom surface of the beetle was a mass of short legs, all gripped tightly to the vine.

Wayland, when faced with an intricate problem to solve, did one of three things; pass it to someone else, don't do it, or hit it with a large object. Looking around he saw only Wayland, who looked busy. The vine was looking very distressed, so it needed doing, which left only option three. He picked up a fallen branch and swung it with all his might. The branch shattered against the knife ridge on the beetles back. As he stood holding the shattered remains, the beetle slowly withdrew its legs, then dropped off the vine, landing upside down in the soil with a loud thud.

"Aha! Brains overcome animal instinct. You know, lying there like that it almost looks like a lobster." Said Wayland.

"Yes, it does, ummm, but how do we cook it?" Answered Wayland.

"We can just barbecue it. Get a fire going and roast it."

"Sounds good," replied Wayland, "But how are we going to start a fire?"

"I'm glad you asked me that, because it just so happens I have a lighter with me, in case we bumped into one of those plants with the very large leaves." Wayland winked knowingly.

"You know, you think of everything, you're a very smart guy."

"Thank you, not so bad yourself."

"Only, I have noticed you've been talking to yourself for sometime, do you think we may be in need of food and water?"

"I think you're right, if we eat this lobster thing, perhaps we'll feel better."

"Ok jump to it then." finished Wayland.

Wayland walked over to the still inverted beetle and carefully got hold of it. Gently he tried to lift it, but nothing happened, it wouldn't budge. He then heaved with all his might, this time just managing to get the animal out of the hole it had made when it fell. "I must be weaker than I thought." He said as he carried it onto a piece of flat ground. In what looked a likely spot he dropped the beetle upside down onto the soft ground. It made another hole, immobilising it until he could gather some fuel.

He had piled a large mound of wood together when he noticed the creature was no longer in its hole. He wasn't sure how it got out, but sure enough, tracks lead away from it. Examining the tracks made him rather angry, they were the same ones he had followed to get into this mess.

Grabbing a stick from the pile, he began to follow the tracks. The heavy beetle had travelled a surprising distance, it took Wayland several minutes to catch up. After a few experimental bonks with the stick, Wayland finally had to face up to Man's modern-day dilemma; have I got the nerve to kill it myself? In this ready-prepared, chilled food age, where nobody killed anything any more, except the butchers, who could ever imagine themselves taking life just for food? Marlo once told him that if people had to hunt for themselves, the numbers of vegetarians would triple overnight. Wayland looked around for any sign of edible fruits or plants, then, seeing none, he battered the living crap out of the beetle. Marlo talked a load of bollocks sometimes.

The lobster beetle, as he had now re-named it, cooked beautifully in its own shell. It did taste like lobster, a little anyway, but with a more nutty taste. He was now walking through the trees with the shell perched on his head. It made a lovely hat, if he said so himself, and fitted a treat. The beetle had filled his stomach but was a little low on juices. His lips were cracked and his mouth was very dry. He knew if he didn't get water soon he would be very ill.

At that thought, the sound of running water drifted down to his ears. But, he thought, if the water is running down, why isn't it running down here? See, I'm smarter than I look. I know an illumination when I see one. Wayland carried on walking, his feet dragging through the leaf litter. Besides, he continued, I'm perfectly all right, I can go days yet without water. Still, it wouldn't hurt to have a look, perhaps there are more lobster beetles up there. With great effort Wayland crawled up the steep hill on all fours.

Half way up, the hill levelled off, revealing a wide pool of clear water surrounded by low bushes. Higher up, a slim waterfall dropped twenty metres into the lower pool. Although the pool was filled to the rim none of the water over-flowed. "Wow!" gasped Wayland, "If you' re going to have one, have a big one. When I illuminate I sure do it in style." He crawled closer, along a flat rock that tilted its far edge just under the surface. His hands dipped into the cool water, sending a tingle up his arm. Cautiously he lifted some of the clear liquid in cupped hands and brought it to his lips.

After a second handful he sat back, "Well, you've got to hand it to me, my illuminations even taste real." He stood up, somewhat refreshed by the phantom water, and walked towards the rim of the hill. "Besides," he continued, "I'm perfectly all right, I can go days yet without water." With that he pitched head first into one of the low bushes. "I wonder if this thing is poisonous?" Wayland said through a mouthful of hairy leaves, then passed out.

He awoke sometime later, the sun was shining gently through the leaves of a palm tree. To his left a tall naked woman wafted a large fan back and forth ... "Hold it." Shouted Wayland. "A tall naked woman on a lush tropical beach, I don't think so. Take it all away and bring reality back."

Reluctantly, the woman stood and walked slowly out of the picture, turning into Dr Crippen. The palm tree grew wings like a giant dragonfly and flittered away. A yellow fruit shaped like an aerobics instructor's bottom hovered enticingly near his mouth. "And you, I don't want any of that floydian crap in my deranged ramblings."

But the fruit wouldn't move, no matter how he tried. So, he decided to wake up and investigate. Sure enough, the fruit was real, it had rolled into the crush of leaves made by his head. Just as an experiment Wayland rolled over and tried to sit up. Everything went fine until he heard the sound of running water. "Not you again," he said to the waterfall and pool, "I thought I told you to get lost?" Wayland rubbed his eyes, then his forehead and temples, then his nuts. When he looked again the water was still there. "Well, I guess you must be real then, but if I dive into you and hit my head on reality, I'll be very angry."

Actually, Wayland was in no state to be leaping about, so he rolled towards the pool and sort of slipped in. The water was cold on his sweaty skin, it took his breath and woke him up. He drank deeply, trying not to think what else he might be taking in. If a green thing started growing in his gut at least he could go on tele, on "Freak of the Week' or something.

After a refreshing drink and a paddle around, he decided he was hungry. Having tested the defensive capabilities of the low bush by head-butting it, he felt confident enough to pick several of the fist sized fruits. They seemed to start off as a dark green colour, then ripen to white, through several stages of yellow. Breaking one open, he discovered a fleshy, squash ball like seed in the middle. The seed bounced quite well when he threw it, nearly taking his eye out on the return.

Now he had stopped talking to himself, probably due to the drink he'd had, Wayland had the sense not to eat the fruit straight away, but to observe other local fauna, to see what their reaction was.

Three hours later something finally turned up. He had forgotten how little actually movable wildlife there was. He had returned to the tilted rock and was lying with his feet in the water when a rustling caught his ear. Turning towards the sound he saw a small, long legged rat like creature with a long beak. The bird rat, as Wayland immediately christened it, picked its way among the greenery with delicate steps, making a twittering whistley type noise. The creature examined several of the fallen fruits before deciding on a medium sized yellow one. It then stepped over the fruit, lowered its belly on to it and stood up. The fruit had disappeared. Wayland's eyes goggled. Had the bird rat just bypassed its mouth and pushed the fruit straight into its stomach? Or was there a fold of skin under the fur which held the fruit whilst the thing moved somewhere safer?

Deciding he didn't know, and not knowing whether the animal had actually eaten the fruit, he was forced to wait for something else. He had another drink to damp down his hunger, then settled down again.

He had just got to the good part of a fantasy involving two gym instructors and a weight bench, when a loud crackle made him jump. From behind the bush a strange creature shaped like a snooker cue pushed its way to the pool. The fat end hung over the water and began to drink noisily. As it filled up, the thin end swelled until it resembled a cucumber. The cue-snake, as Wayland named it, crackled again, then made its way back to the bushes. This animal was nowhere near as fussy as the last, it simply sucked in the fruits as it came to them, until a set of them could been seen inside it. Looking like an inflated novelty condom, the cue-snake slithered away.

Right, thought Wayland, that's enough. He leapt up, gathered up a good dozen different colours, then returned to the rock. In a film he had once seen, a Chick Nodule film called 'Enter the Back Way,' the hero, Throb Hammerdong, had been marooned on a tiny island by Loos lee Pakt, the arch-criminal and terminally stupid bad guy. I mean, why not just blow Throb's brains all over the furniture? You know he'll come back and nearly kill you, then you'll try to trick him and then he will kill you but you deserve it because of what you did to that ferret and those nuns. But no, you just stick him on this island inhabited by small ethnic under-dogs who he can train to become hard, son of a bitch fighting machines.

Anyway, Throb's on this island, on his own at first. He can't find anything to eat, so he watches these monkeys picking fruit, then he picks the same type. Then, and this is the clever bit, he breaks a bit off, licks it, then waits. He doesn't drop to the floor, mouth foaming, eyes rolling, so he eats a bit. When he isn't violently sick or shitting brown porridge, he eats some more. That way he knows they are safe.

Wayland selected a nice firm white one and peeled it. The flesh smelled strongly of beer, a nutty, hoppy sort of smell, like real ale. The cloudy juice began to run down his fingers, without thinking he quickly caught the drips on his tongue. The juice tasted sweet, like fruit should, tasting vaguely of strawberry jelly, but with a custardy after taste. What the hell, thought Wayland, and sunk his teeth into it. Flavour burst on his tongue, like eating a particularly tangy trifle, all mixed together. Making that noise people make when they are enjoying something, that 'ummm' sound, he finished off the fruit in a few more bites.

The taste had been so nice he grabbed another one, yellow this time, and bit straight into it. He was very surprised to find the fruit tasted completely different. This yellow one had the consistency of fruit but the flavour of beef, in peanut and ale sauce. He tried another, this time a yellowy green. This one was very similar to the last, but less peanutty. Finally he tested a green one. Most surprisingly of all this tasted like tomato and was very juicy.

I was going to call this a snooker bush, but I think dinner bush is better, thought Wayland. He suddenly realised he hadn't used the Throb Hammerdong Survival Technique, in his excitement he had forgotten all about it. Well, I'll just sit here quietly and see what happens.

Several minutes passed, the only thing to happen was he felt a little sleepy, but I've just eaten, he thought, I always used to sleep after a meal, even at work, after a tea-break. He settled down for a nap, the waterfall splashing happily not far away.

Chapter Eight

Up and Down

Wayland's booted feet trudged along a rough tarmac road. In his left hand a battered and stained suitcase hung from its knotted rope handle. He shivered inside his travel stained overcoat, hugging it closed with his right hand against the driving sleet. Icy fingers from the incessant wind sought out every tear and mend in his threadbare trousers. On his grimy face, among the creases of his determined smile, a single tear formed a salty trail.

Echoing footsteps filled the silence of the grey buildings all around. Brown doors and peeling windows challenged him to enter, but resolutely he walked on, up the narrow hill towards the single point of light in the dim morning. Finally, after many years away, he stood hesitantly before the house that had been his home for all his childhood years. His first knock was quiet, almost silent, a tap. Gathering his courage he wiped away the tear, threw his shoulders back and knocked again, this time more confident, as befitted the man he had become.

After what seemed like many minutes, during which his resolve began to slowly ebb away, the sound of keys turning reached out through the yellowing u.P.V.C. The door opened a crack, then wider, revealing the face of a middle-aged woman, hard work engrained in her every feature.

"What!" She said loudly, looking Wayland up and down.

"Hello Mum." Answered Wayland, voice trembling.

"Who are you?" The woman asked.

"It's me, Wayland." Said Wayland.

"Wayland Who?" She demanded suspiciously, flicking her fag end at a passing dog.

"You know, Wayland, your son."

The woman's eyes widened in sudden recognition. "Oh, that Wayland. Hello son. It's no use coming in, I've let your room. Might as well piss off." With that she coughed, spat a nicotine coloured lump into the gutter, and slammed the door.

* * * *

Wayland awoke as a shiver ran down his spine. The rock had grown cold while he slept, the sun dipping rapidly towards dusk. That dream again, he thought, he hadn't had that one in ages, he thought he had got rid of it. Must have been the strain. Several variations of the dream had come and gone since he had joined this colony mission and shipped out, but they all ended the same. The sad thing was the ending was true. When he had got back from two years away at university, where he'd been failing a business and finance course, that's exactly what had happened.

Sighing, he stood and looked around. The jungle at the bottom of the hill was already dark, he didn't like the idea of going down there. Looking up the hill he could see the last few sunbeams lighting the top. The hill was very steep, but Wayland felt he could manage it now, in his recently nourished form.

Hand over hand, step by step, he determinedly climbed the slippery greenery foliage that smothered the hill. At last, wheezing like an ex lab beagle, he dropped down on level ground. After several minutes of deep breathing Wayland had the strength to look around. What had looked like the summit from down below was actually just a wide platform. The hill itself continued steeply up another few hundred feet.

Spotting some sensor vines hanging down from the heights, Wayland decided to spend the night in those and explore further later. He dragged his weary lungs over to the cliff face and slumped into a loop of vine. The sun had set further during his mountaineering, the last rays of light were quickly fading. Just in time, thought Wayland, climbing to seven point six metres above the ground. Sensor vines clutched him all around, his full stomach gurgled nicely, and his weary but replete body settled to sleep.

Wayland slowly peeled his eyelids open some hours later. All was dark. Not the dark of night with its twinkling stars and flickering shadows, but the deep, endless black of oblivion. "Oh my god I've been eaten alive by some terrible but as yet undiscovered new species, that inhabits the darker regions of this planet." Actually he only thought that, he really screamed, "Oh shit!"

For several moments a panic gripped him like a lift door. Then the sensor vines behind him slowly unwound, letting sunshine stream into a large cave. Wayland swung his head around, first one way, then the other. Outside, a cool breeze was blowing in an early morning sort of a way. Inside, warm air wafted against his face.

Not believing what he saw, Wayland untangled himself from the vines and climbed down. From what he could see the cave was quite deep and high, and completely hidden by the vines, until now of course. The curtain of growth had parted during the night, from top to bottom, leaving a gap he could walk through and letting plenty of light in.

It was almost as if the vines had opened just for him, and that whilst he slept the vines had turned him around so that he would see the cave.

In the deep uncharted region of Wayland's mind, where thoughts never went, and psychiatrists feared to tread, on the barren, featureless plain of Wayland's initiative, two ideas, passing in opposite directions, collided. The resultant pile-up, a million to one freak accident, caused a tremor that ran all the way across the plains into the one-way system of Wayland's logic. The tremor, maturing nicely into a realisation, shot passed a slip road, backed up, and headed down onto the M25 of thought processors that was Wayland's brain. It would be here for some time.

Wayland pulled out his trusty laser measurer and shone it into the cave. A spot of light appeared nine point three metres away on a greyish stone wall. His eyes slowly adjusted to the gloom of the cave, revealing walls that curved to his right, and into the darkness. The walls were seven point seven metres apart, and a quick measurement from the floor put the ceiling at precisely the same height. The floor was smooth, clean and flat, almost manmade, thought Wayland. Although the walls looked like unworked stone, they were very regular.

Now Wayland wasn't the bravest man you would ever meet, even at a coward's convention, but he wasn't the brightest of people either. Thus, the two tended to cancel out, making him appear quite reckless on occasion. So, keeping to the wall to allow the sunlight in, he crept into the cave as far as the light would allow. Due to the grey walls, which reflected some of the light, this was quite a distance. Just around the corner, the cave was shaped like a shallow spiral, it opened up into a circular area that the light barely touched.

A light of some kind was needed, thought Wayland. He went back out into the brightening day and looked around for something to set fire to. After an hour or so of dashing back and forth he had constructed a crude torch made of wood and some dry grassy stuff. He lit it with his lighter, swore when he realised he could have just used his lighter, then swore again as the torch burnt to nothing in less than four seconds.

This time, Wayland went as far as the beams of sunlight, then held up his lighter and carried on around. The small circular area was a perfect circle seven point seven metres across. The area wasn't just circular, it was actually a sphere, as Wayland worked out all by himself.

There was no sign of animal life here at all, not even the scrotes, who would live anywhere, had found this place. Well, he thought, this looks like a nice place for a spot of camping until I'm rescued. Going back out, he gathered several bundles of the dry grass and numerous large sticks. He also found a very large leaf that looked familiar, so he collected that too.

Now he was in two minds whether to sleep with some security at the back of the cave, or some comfort on the wall of vines. In the end, and after trying the cave floor, which seemed very warm, he settled for the cave.

Breakfast, his stomach said loudly. Wayland realised gloomily that there was no food or water up here. Which meant a climb down the hill every time he wanted to eat or drink. His stomach grumbled loudly, giving Wayland no choice but to scramble down the mountainside as best he could.

Landing without too much embarrassment, he set about gathering fruits from the three-course bush, as he had re-named it. After breakfast he had a long drink, a quick wash, then set off back up the hill with his shirt stuffed with fruit. He got to the top without squashing too many, which he stored in the cave. Realising he would still have to go down for water, he slapped his head, then looked around for a container. When he had found nothing suitable and was sitting on the hill thinking sad thoughts, he suddenly remembered the lobster bug shell. The last time he'd seen it was when he had it on his head. Thinking back, he recalled how he had dropped it whilst rushing up the hill to investigate the sound of running water.

Which meant it was down there, in the jungle somewhere, probably surrounded by all its relatives, talking revenge and cooking up plots to eat him alive. You really must get a grip on that imagination, he thought, but didn't make a move towards the jungle. Wayland agreed with himself that it would do him good to fetch water when he needed it, so might as well get fresh fruit too.

The next day, whilst swimming in the cool lake, he looked up at the waterfall. He realised he hadn't explored it, or tried to find where the water came from, or went to for that matter. Taking the latter thought first, Wayland swam all around the edge of the pool looking for an outlet. Five minutes later he found it under the flat rock he used to dry himself in the sun. A series of irregular holes drained the water into the hill itself. No wonder there was no water running down the slope.

Later, when he returned to the cave, he leaned over the hill above the waterfall. The water emerged from a narrow crack in the rock face, but it was too far out of his reach to save him a climb down.

At night, Wayland had noticed, the vines closed over the cave mouth, as though they knew he needed the security of a closed space. He settled down to sleep for another night, curling up on the curved floor, shuffling around until he got comfy.

Meanwhile, on the M25, the realisation flashed its lights and honked its horn to grab the attention of a passing thought riding a vine-shaped motor-cycle. The thought slowed, waved then zoomed off.

Lying alone in the darkness, Wayland started thinking about Sonia and the rest of the crew. They had certainly spared all expense coming to look for him. No sign of rescue shuttles or robot drones. No one scouring the area for him. Well, what did I expect, he thought, it's just the usual thing, my life in the toilet by Wayland U. Snowball. Grumbling and mumbling to himself, he fell into a deep sleep.

Outside, a search droid hung in the air scanning the area for the tell-tale signs of movement and the heat of human bodies. The sensor vines quite adequately screened any heat from the cave, and the sound of efficient whisper-quiet motors was almost perfectly cancelled out by the splashing of water into the pool. Finding nothing to report, the droid moved on to the next sector.

That night Wayland began to dream, deep meaningful dreams, about philosophical subjects; unstoppable forces and lengths of string, about whole body awareness and the ultimate uselessness of existence. It frightened the crap out of him.

Several days later Wayland had got into something of a routine. He went down the slope for breakfast when he woke up, which was usually just after sunrise. Then he swam in the pool, first with and then without his clothes, after which he laid his only garments on the rock to dry. Later, as the sun set, he gathered a shirt full of fruits, took a long drink and walked back up to his cave.

Strangely, the mountain he had scrambled up the first few days didn't seem as steep now. He was easily able to walk up it without stopping halfway like he used to. And, he could walk back down using just his legs, instead of sliding on his backside. Wayland attributed this to the hill eroding away as he went up and down each day.

On this particular day he arrived at the top of the hill as usual, with the sun just starting to sink into the west. But as he walked towards the sensor vines, which stood open, a thought loomed up out of nowhere. The thought, which had stolen a forty ton truck from an overweight synapse and had been driving around Wayland's M25 for days, finally had him in his sights. It floored the gas pedal and aimed straight for Wayland's conscious mind, a small wooden shed of the kind kids find hardly worth even vandalising. The thought roared across the barren tarmac, smashing into the shed with such impact it split into kindling that was shot for miles in all directions.

Wayland stood transfixed, staring at the vines. As the wreckage settled, reforming itself, the thought had lodged well and truly into his mind. "The sensor vines react to emotional need, not just physical presence. That's why they moved around me when I slept. Wow! Think what this could mean! Er … Yes, I could do party tricks." He walked over to the curtain of vines and reached out his hand, thinking he wanted to touch the vine. Nothing happened. Right, he thought, let's try this. Wayland wanted to touch the vine, he needed to, he needed proof that he wasn't going mad out here.

As the emotion welled up in his head the vine moved, several stems writhed and pushed out loops towards him, until they touched his hand. Wayland was gob-smacked. He didn't have a clue how they did it, nor did he even care, but it was a neat trick, something to show he hadn't wasted his time out here when he was finally rescued. He entered the cave and walked into his little den. The vines obediently closed behind him as soon as he had banked up his fire enough to see.

Later, as he got comfortable on the curved floor, he thought about the dreams he had been having, they had been very weird. He wondered if it was some effect of his diet, perhaps a chemical in the fruit, or a deficiency of some vitamin. Whatever it was, the dreams were certainly funny, from Wayland's point of view at least. They only link he had been able to find was the fact that if he slept nearer the centre of the sphere, the stranger the dreams. Possibly the blood went to his head at that angle, which could mean there was something wrong with his blood. He vowed to go down into the jungle and find something else to eat. Tomorrow. Or the day after.

The next morning it rained, massive, head battering raindrops that bounced when they hit the ground. This kept up for several hours, during which Wayland paced up and down, eager to get out on his daily run. At last, a few hours before dusk, the rain eased off.

The path down to the pool was slick with water, but to his surprise Wayland made it without once falling over. Quickly he gathered up as many fruits as he could find, drunk so much water he was nearly sick, then ran back up the hill. The clouds returned a few minutes later, big chunky black ones. That one looks like a milk bottle, thought Wayland. And that one is the spitting image of my aunt Fanny. That one's two slugs having it off. And that one looks like the Chinese symbol of yin and yang, twisted through ninety degrees. Wayland froze. Where the hell did that thought come from? What was he doing looking at clouds anyway? Get inside you fool, before you get wet.

Wayland was now very worried, he had never before thought such soft things would enter his mind, he'd be picking flowers next, and making his own dresses. Yin and yang? He hadn't thought anything about that since he was shown it by Mr Tucox, his English teacher, It was a Wednesday afternoon, about two o'clock. He was sitting next to the boy who was to become famous by screwing the headmistress and all three of her daughters on the same weekend. Richard Phytan, nick name 'Python Dick'. Wayland froze again. Yes, so remember a few details, not the whole damn day. Now he was seriously distressed. He had to get out of here before he cracked up all together. Tomorrow, when it's bright enough I'm going to light a fire, a big fuck off fire that can be seen miles away. With that, he settled down to sleep, with his head as far away from the centre as possible.

Chapter Nine

You Lucky Bastard

A lone figure strode across the rain-lashed jungle floor. The wind blew water into the figure's eyes, forcing him to turn his face. The mud squelched and oozed as he doggedly placed one foot in front of another. Suddenly, to his left, a tall creature arose, leaping to attack with its overlong fingers. The figure didn't even look in its direction, merely lashed out with his clenched fist. The blow hit the creature under its low chin, sending it screaming backwards into a puddle of purplish liquid, sprawling on its six limbs. Several other figures huddled in the darkness, but none dared to approach.

At last the figure reached the relative safety of a run-down compound. The laser fence was working, after a fashion, although there were many gaps along its length. The man touched a finger to a scratched keypad. Many tries later the gate accepted his I.D. and allowed him to enter. Now, the man walked hesitantly, approaching the habitat he had left two cycles before.

A battered metal door stood before him, quietly he tapped against the steel. The sound of locks being deactivated reached through the door several minutes later. A woman's face peered around the door, a nicotine patch practically welded to her forehead.

"Yes, what do you want?" She screeched.

"It's me mum, Wayland."

"Wayland? Oh, that Wayland. Piss off, we've let your pod." The woman started to close the door.

"I didn't come here to ask to come back. I came to tell you I am leaving, I've been selected to go on a colony mission. All expenses paid, luxury cabin to a new world. You can keep my stuff, I might write to you when I get there, see you."

With that the figure turned and walked away into the sunset.

The woman watched him go, then slowly, carefully, closed the door.

* * * *

Wayland woke in a strangely triumphant mood. He had forgotten the dream almost immediately on waking, but the feeling of euphoria persisted. He leapt up, took several deep breaths, pulled on his trousers and headed for the entrance. He skipped along, singing as he went.

"My father lies over the ocean,

My mother lies over the sea,

My brother lies over my sister,

There's incest in our family."

The vines opened as he approached, rattling wildly, picking up his high spirits. Wayland stepped lightly down the hill, jumping from rock to turf, turf to soil, enjoying the feel of the sun on his skin.

As he reached a large bush that over hung the pool, by seven point nine two metres, he heard a splash in the water. His mood went from happy to miserable in one step. Here we go again, he thought, head back down the toilet. Silently he moved over to the bush and slowly moved back the branches. A pink shape appeared out of the water, stood for a few seconds, then dived back in. Wayland used the noise to move further into the bush. He now had an almost clear view over the pool. A shape moved under the water, then a head popped out by his sunning rock. The figure had long blonde hair, and was quite slender. Knowing my luck, thought Wayland, it's a Swedish male jockey.

Leaning a little closer to get a better view, Wayland saw the figure slowly emerge from the water and turn around. The woman was very attractive, with blue eyes, a small nose and full lips. The water ran down her golden locks, between large firm breasts and down past her slim waist. She had a tight bottom and a small triangle of light pubic hair. Her legs were long, well proportioned and graceful. All in all a vision of beauty.

Of course Wayland didn't think these thoughts, his were more along the lines of; "Look at the tits on that!" And "Fu-ckin-hell, she's got no knickers on and I can see her minge." He leaned closer for a better view. The jelly effect dropped in with a vengeance. Wayland looked at the whip-thin branch in front of him and thought, of course it will hold me. He grabbed hold of it and leaned out. The twig, naturally, snapped like a cheap video tape, sending him arse over tit into the pool.

A vague image of something pink rushing backwards, reached his retina as the water came up to meet him. With a very ungainly splat he disappeared into the cool depths. When he surfaced and looked around the vision had gone, to be replaced by a young woman wearing a one-piece zip fronted suit, and holding a small but decidedly menacing weapon.

"Er ... hello, mind if I drop in." Stammered Wayland. To his infinite surprise, the woman smiled. A bright, sunny smile that ripped its way through Wayland's ribcage and savaged his heart.

"Who are you? And what are you doing out here?" She asked without a hint of fright or threat, though she still held the gun.

"Well, I er ... got lost actually, well, not lost, separated. I was with a scientific survey group. My name's Wayland, Wayland Snowball." He waited for the laugh.

"Pleased to meet you Wayland, why don't you climb out and get dried." She held out her hand to help him, no laugh, just a warm smile on her face.

When he had climbed out, the two sat on the rock in the sun to dry off.

"My name's Honee, by the way." They shook hands. Wayland found it very difficult to let go of the warm, soft touch. "So, how long have you been lost, sorry, separated from your group?" Honee asked.

"Actually, I'm not sure, two or three weeks, possibly

longer. I suppose I'll get round to finding them one day."

Honee looked very surprised, "You've been out here three weeks? That's amazing. And you've managed to survive, you look very well I must say."

Wayland was dumb-struck, a gorgeous woman saying he looked well? That's a first, they usually said 'get lost loony' or something similar. Self-consciously he raised his hand to his face and touched the scar. Honee noticed straight away. "How did you do that? It looks quite painful." She was genuinely concerned.

"Oh, this is nothing, my own fault really. It doesn't hurt now. It was some kind of plant, a new discovery apparently."

Honee smiled widely, "Wow, how exciting," She gushed, "It must be nice to have a job like that, finding new species on a new planet like this. What have you been eating out here, I suppose you know all the plants by name."

"Not all of them," Wayland said truthfully, "But if you'd like to try a few, I'm sure I could find you something."

"Really? Actually eat wild berries and things, that would be great." Smiled Honee excitedly.

Wayland was unsure whether she was real, if she was faking it she was a very good actress, or just a fig leaf of my imagination, he thought. But she felt solid enough. Mind you, so did he at the moment. He hoped his clothes would hide the bulge as he stood up.

He led her over to one of the bushes, which luckily were still full of fruits. Picking one of each colour, he handed them to her. "Now, eat this green one first, then the yellows and then the white." He explained. "I call it the three-course-bush." He said as she ate.

"They're very nice, really sweet and juicy. I don't think I've ever eaten anything native before. How did you know they weren't poisonous?" Honee asked.

Wayland smiled casually, "It's quite straight forward really, just common sense, you know, watch the animals, taste the juice first, that sort of thing."

"That's wonderful," she gushed, "You really are smart aren't you?"

Wayland blushed deep red and turned away. The last woman to say that to him was getting paid to say it, among other things. "I'll show you where I've been staying, come on it's this way." Leading on, he began to climb the hill. About half-way up Honee began to get out of breath. Heroically, Wayland reached for her hand and helped her up the rest of the way. Her warm skin against his set him throbbing all over again. Glad now that he had gone up and down this slope at least once a day, he showed off by not being winded when they reached the summit. She seemed suitably impressed.

The vines moved to one side when Wayland approached. Honee gasped as they made an entry for him.

"How do they do that? I thought they just sensed human presence, how did they know you were going in?"

"Oh, they can read emotions, I just think I need to go in and they open up."

"You mean they're actually empathic?"

"Er, yes I suppose they are." Empathic, must look up empathic, thought Wayland.

He lead Honee around the slight curve and into his ball-shaped cave. Again, she gasped when she saw it. "Wayland, you mean you've spent almost a month in this cave, you poor thing, however did you manage it? There must be more to you than meets the eye." She looked at him steadily, as though trying to work out his hidden depths. Which wasn't actually very difficult. Take a sheet of paper and lay it flat, there, that's his depth of character, and that's after a month of character building basic survival.

Wayland shrugged, he was a man of simple needs, by force mostly. He hadn't expected it to be any different, the way his luck went. Noticing Honee was smiling to herself, he checked his flies, then asked her what she was smiling at.

"Oh, I was just wondering what it would be like, you know, to stay here for a few days."

"You're welcome to try it, for a few days, or as long as you like." Wayland stuttered out hurriedly.

"All right, this is going to be fun."

Yes, thought Wayland, let's hope so. His eyes lit up lasciviously. Honee didn't seem to notice. "Right, shall we go and get some more of those fruits to eat, I'm starving." She smiled one of her mind-numbing smiles and Wayland grinned like an idiot, nodding eagerly. She might have said, "Let's go and tie your gonads to a horse and then make it run away really fast." He would have smiled and nodded just the same.

After a bite to eat and a quick swim, in their underwear to Wayland's regret, they returned to the cave. They spent the rest of the day gathering the soft grassy stuff that he had been sleeping on and making the cave fit for two. The fire was banked up ready for dusk, and several of the fruits had been stored. Wayland noticed that Honee had built her bed on the opposite side of the fire to his, well, there was plenty of room next to him, if she chose to move.

Later that night they settled down to sleep, Wayland's stiffy pumping in anticipation. Honee laid on her bed and closed her eyes. "It's been a long and interesting day," she said softly, "I hope tomorrow is just as good."

"Yes, me too." Sighed Wayland.

"Wayland?" said Honee quietly.

"Yes?" he said eagerly.

"Goodnight."

"Goodnight." He replied, trying not to sound disappointed.

As Wayland drifted into sleep, his mind numb from the faint smell of woman in the close cave, he suddenly realised he didn't know where the hell she had come from. She had just appeared in the middle of the jungle, as if from thin air. It didn't matter now, let her sleep. I'll ask her tomorrow. A noise somewhere next to him awoke him suddenly. He sat up quickly to find Honee leaning over him. Yes! Thought Mr Stiffy, we're going in, and began to prepare, mainly by going hard.

"Oh, you're already awake, I didn't sleep very well, so I've been up for a while. I just wondered if you were ready for breakfast?" she walked back to her bed and sat down.

Damn, thought Mr Stiffy, mission aborted.

"Yes, ready when you are, I'm usually up with the sun." Which was true lately, but a blatant lie up until a month ago, when he thought six o'clock only happened once a day, in the evening. They walked hand in hand down the slope to the pool and ate the fruits for breakfast. Wayland started the day with dark green ones, which had a lighter taste. Honee copied, Wayland thought this very cute.

After breakfast Honee turned to Wayland and said, "Shall we go for a swim? The water looks really nice."

"Yes, ok" They began to undress.

Wayland was down to his undies when he realised Honee had removed her bra and was pulling down her pants. Quickly he snatched off his shorts, and dived into the pool, just in time to slow down, but not stop, his dick leaping up like a manic rabbit on speed. He surfaced just in time to see Honee's tits disappear into the water.

Several minutes of small talk and splashing around followed, the pair finally ending up leaning against the sunning rock. Wayland swam over to join them, her. "I wonder where the water goes? If it comes out up there at this rate all the time it must go somewhere." She looked around, giving Wayland a glimpse of her dark nipples.

"It er, it goes through a hole under this rock and down into the hill. " He said as casually as he could. Honee looked at him strangely, then pulled herself out, stretching out flat to dry in the sun. "You are a unique man Wayland," she said, looking him in the eye. "You pretend to be a clown, falling in the water and making up names for bushes, but deep down you are very clever and resourceful, you obviously studied this place, to find the cave and where the water goes, and even to survive this long out here. I've never met a man who could spend the night in a lonely cave with a woman and stay on his side of the fire. Most men I meet try it on straight away."

Wayland felt himself blushing again. He ducked under the water for a cooling drink, then pulled himself out onto the rock, carefully laying on his throbbing member to hide it. He was desperately trying not to tell Honee the truth about himself, and wondered why he felt so bad about it. Usually, he would tell any lie he could palm off as truth to get into a girl's knickers.

He tried to change the subject, to deflate Dick Williams as much as to stop himself talking. "You know, I never asked about you, where you came from, how you managed to be in my pool and all that."

"That's right you didn't, another thing about you, you're very trusting, a girl likes that in a man. I came here in my shuttle, my father is looking for a sight to build a brewery, but with all this vegetation, which we aren't allowed to harm of course, land is very rare, and expensive. I was scouting around when I saw this open space. I scanned for life forms, found nothing but microbes, and so decided to have a closer look. It's quite unsuitable of course, but it was so inviting after days in the shuttle, I couldn't resist a swim. And of course I met you, which was very lucky."

"You … your father owns a brewery? Very interesting." Stammered Wayland, completely ignoring the fact that a shuttle was standing somewhere close by, ready to lead him back to civilisation. In his mind a thought raised its head. A gorgeous woman whose father owns a brewery? It's a dream, I'll wake up any minute. There's something in the fruit, a lucy jenic chemical. Must be, when do I ever get this kind of luck?

A few moments later he realised Honee was still talking.

"… for some time now, I suppose he's training me to take over, but I'm not sure I'm ready yet. What does your father do?"

"Oh, he used to be in the removals business, (removing things from peoples houses when they were out, he thought) but I think he's retired now, I haven't seen my parents in years. They still live on Earth."

Several minutes of silence followed, then Honee spoke softly, "Wayland, I know what you're laying on, and I'm really flattered. You don't have to hide it, I don't mind."

Wayland blushed from head to toe, he couldn't remember blushing so much in his life. But slowly and with some relief, he rolled onto his back. Sure enough, Mr bone was still ready to play.

"You've got nothing to be ashamed of, you're quite the equal of others I've seen." Honee moved next to him and began to kiss the scar on his face, then moved over to his lips. Her kiss sent pulses down his entire body, making his heart beat faster, his dick throb quicker. She moved further and brushed her nipples over his arm and against his chest. The effect was electric, Wayland moaned softly, tingles racing up and down his body. He reached out, running his hands over the soft skin on her back, tracing the line of her back bone, she groaned sensuously. Honee thrust her tongue between Wayland's lips, tasting the fruit juices from the breakfast feast. Eagerly Wayland returned her kiss, their tongues rolling around each other like courting eels.

Then Honee pulled away and began kissing his chest, down his stomach and along his leg. Wayland moaned again, all the while thinking don't come yet, don't come yet, chanting it over and over. She carried on down his leg to his knee then began to move up again, this time on the inside. Wayland groaned loudly, his hands gripping and opening, his legs slowly moving apart. Her tongue reached his testicles. Lightly her tongue passed over his left ball, up his hard shaft, then back down to his right one. Wayland groaned deeper, louder, then shot his load straight into his belly button.

Honee looked up at his suddenly still form. "Oh," she said, noticing the small puddle. "Sorry, I forgot you've been out here a while, perhaps I shouldn't have been so ambitious. Never mind we can try again later." Honee laid down next to a stunned Wayland. The last time he'd done that the woman had slapped him and thrown him out. Then again he had been trying on jeans in a clothes shop. Now, along comes Honee and she's perfectly understanding. Something told Wayland to hang on to this woman; obviously wealthy, very considerate and a father with a brewery, almost a perfect combination.

A few hours later, and several times after that, they did indeed try again, with Wayland keeping his end up much better. Honee was a noisy finisher, so to speak, which Wayland loved. Having heard Sonia orgasming he knew what to expect this time around. They had sex in the pool and on the rock, in the cave and on the hill, in several different positions, most of which were new to Wayland, he had never been fit enough to do it standing up before.

But finally, as these things do, the shag-fest came to an end, as Wayland punned later. Honee decided she had been away long enough, and had to report to her father. As the shuttle was only large enough for one she offered to radio ahead to the jungle station, to inform them of his position. (They both giggled at that one.) He gladly accepted, he hadn't realised until now how much he'd missed the comforts of civilisation; a soft bed, proper food, and lots of beer.

The next morning, following a night of oral sex, Wayland and Honee set off into the jungle to find her shuttle. The white and grey craft soon came into site perched on a small bald hill about ten minutes walk away. Although Wayland was no expert when it came to aircraft, he could tell it was expensive. It was bright and sleek, shaped like an elongated cone sat on three legs. It wasn't very big for a shuttle, but even so it filled the hill on which it stood, more or less level. Wayland was glad that there was insufficient flat ground on his hill to land the craft, if he'd heard Honee set this thing down, it might have turned out differently, she might have took straight off again on seeing his face grinning up at her.

"I am really sorry it's not big enough for two, there's only one seat and some storage space, the rest is engine and control systems. But I can radio your friends as soon as I'm above the trees, then when you get back to your base you can call me, O.K?" Wayland nodded as Honee hugged him, planting a big kiss on his lips. "I'll miss you, you know? But hopefully not for too long. I'll see you when I've visited dad."

They embraced for several minutes. Wayland glad that

no one could see him being so soppy. Finally they broke apart. Honee led them around the shuttle, checking everything was as it should be, then, climbing a small ladder set into one of the legs, she touched her hand to a small panel. A door opened just above her and she climbed in. Then she climbed out again, leaned down to give Wayland another kiss, then re-entered the shuttle. Before she closed the door she shouted out, "See you later, don't forget to call, oh, and you'd better move back when the engines ignite, but you know that don't you?"

"Yes, no problem, I'll call when I reach the first phone. Bye!" Before he could stop himself he'd blown her a kiss. Inside something cringed, I hope no one saw that! Honee returned the kiss, then turned to the control panel, "Now then Janet, back to base if you would be so kind." She said clearly. The engines began to whine, blowing out a warm current of air. Wayland stepped back into the trees to watch the shuttle leave. With a final wave Honee closed the door and the craft lifted slowly into the air. It hung above the trees for several seconds, turned around three times and disappeared. Wayland stood in the clearing after it had gone, grinning inanely, a strange warm feeling in his stomach.

He skipped lightly through the jungle, still smiling, thinking nice thoughts, cautiously optimistic. He had now decided that having testicles on the outside was a damn good idea, he'd be leaving them right where they were. Happily Wayland began to sing quietly to himself, a composition of his own, written in his final year at school.

"I love her, you know, but what can I do?

She lives in a paddock down at the zoo.

She's warm and sweet, someone named her Deborah.

She's black and she's white, and I think she's a Zebra."

So it didn't win any prizes, but you've got to start somewhere.

Then reality descended like a DC10, wiping the stupid grin off his face and dropping his jaw to his knees. "Shit!" He shouted emotionally, "Shit!" He shouted again, in case you missed the first one. He looked around and realised he was lost, again.

Chapter Ten

Face first

"Bonk," went Wayland's head against a tree, "Stupid, stupid, stupid, stupid." He said, each time headbutting the tree. The tree, being a tree, didn't complain, but remarked, mainly to itself, how rude young folk were these days.

When this particular method of brain stimulation failed to yield satisfactory results, he stopped, sat down in a loop of vine, and nursed his head. Learn from my previous mistakes, thought Wayland, that's the thing to do. He was sure he could re-trace his steps back to the shuttle landing site, then he could just start again. So, he got up and began to walk. He had been walking for twenty minutes when he realised the journey back should only have taken him ten. He thumped a tree in anger, hurt his hand and felt much worse.

Wayland suddenly remembered that Honee was going to send a message to his base, telling them where he was. Of course, I don't need to go anywhere, I can just wait here, let them do all the work. The droids could find him easily if he just stayed visible. Wayland sat down again in a loop of vine, which he empathically adjusted for comfort. Despite his best effort not to, he smiled when he thought the word 'empathically'.

He was woken sometime later from a light doze by a muffled thumping noise somewhere in the trees behind him. At last, he thought, the droids had found him. He stood up and waited impatiently, hands on hips, chastisement on lips. The bushes in front of him began to tremble and shake, as though something heavy was pushing through them. Moments later a shiny carapace appeared, half concealing an insect like head. The carapace kept on coming until a massive lobster-bug stood a few metres away. Wayland was too dumb struck to measure it exactly.

This thing was easily the size of a small car, even a medium sized one. The narrow head on its long neck emerged fully from the shell, fixing compound eyes on Wayland. Its mouth opened surprisingly wide, revealing rows of needle like teeth. In this position it advanced swiftly towards him, its many legs driving it at quite a speed. Wayland took two or three seconds to recover from his shock, but eventually he turned and ran for his life.

"They don't have large predators here, she said, only small ones, she said, there is nothing dangerous to man out here she said," chanted Wayland as he ran, quoting Sonia. It didn't do any good, the lobster-bug obviously hadn't heard that it didn't exist, or if it did it didn't care. The monster just kept on running, mouth open, legs pumping like little pistons.

Looking ahead Wayland noticed a cloud of white vapour hanging in the air. A shuttle! I'm saved! he thought. But as he drew closer the cloud didn't smell right, it had the odour of tar, not rocket fuel. Nevertheless, he kept on running, perhaps search robots used a different fuel. Wayland hoped to lose the bug in the cloud if it turned out not to be his rescuers.

Getting nearer he managed to add a little speed to his tired legs, reaching the comparative safety of the mist a few seconds ahead of his assailant. He risked a look round, the bug had stopped some metres away, but he wasn't fooled and kept on running. With the mist swirling around him he plunged on through, his arms outstretched to warn him of danger.

Unfortunately it was his feet that found it, or rather lost it. He lost contact with the ground under his feet, went shooting into thin air and landed some seconds later, face first, onto something damp. Good thing I went up and down that hill all those times, or I would never have got away from that bug, he thought sardonically as he lay choking on green slime and vapours. Heat from some unknown source began to creep up his face and feet. Slowly he lifted his head and surveyed his surroundings.

It was difficult to see too far with the fog around, but from what he could see, it would seem he had fallen in a bubbling mud pit, and had landed on the only solid object in it, a fallen tree. Still, he thought, it could have been worse, I could have landed in the mud. No sooner had the thought emerged than the tree trunk began to sink. Well isn't that nice, thought Wayland, somewhat sarcastically, I've managed to discover a type of wood that doesn't float very well.

Dragging himself to his feet, he balanced on the rapidly dwindling log and looked around. A few feet away a long tree root hung over the pit, he could just make out the end of it through the haze. As the mud touched his boots he leapt for the root with all his energy. Desperately, he grabbed at the overhang and clamped his hands as tight as he could around it. His hands, covered with tree slime began to slip, but more alarmingly the root itself began to move. Wayland looked up expecting to see a long forked tongue and two beady eyes looking back at him, but to his relief it was only a sensor vine. Realising with some surprise that the vine was moving him towards the edge of the pit, Wayland concentrated on holding on. A waft of air blew across Wayland's face as he moved, a slight wind had arisen, blowing the fog across the pit. Suddenly, below his feet, he spied a narrow pebbly beach. As the vine swung him over it his hands slipped, dropping him barely onto solid ground.

The increasing wind was blowing the mist away from him here, revealing most of the mud pit to him. Wayland looked up at the vine and smiled, "Thank you," he said to it, "I'll pay you back one day." The vine said nothing, merely rattled slightly. Now he could see more, Wayland realised how lucky he'd been, the fallen log was the only object visible in the bubbling mud, and even that was now sinking. A few minutes later and he'd have been poached.

Now he was safe on solid land, Wayland noticed how pleasant this place was. The shingle beach was forty two metres from end to end and three point three wide. It was backed by a sandy bank on which several types of flower were growing. The pit was twenty point five metres across, give or take a little for the fog dispersing the laser beam. It was roughly oval, its long axis following the beach. The whole thing was surrounded and mostly overhung by trees of different kinds, some of which were in flower. The dominant feature was the mud, it filled the air with the smell of tar and oil, it bubbled noisily, drowning out most other sounds, it left a strange, orangy taste in the mouth. And, here on the bank, it was pleasantly warm.

Wayland turned to walk along the beach, wondering if he could find any three-course-bushes. The bank was one metre ninety six high, which Wayland supposed would keep the lobster bug out, and had several small holes in it, like burrows. A faint humming noise could be heard from some of them, like children singing. He was entranced by the sound, drawn by the pleasant images it conjured. Wayland listened for a moment, but the bubbling of the mud made it difficult to hear. He moved closer, turning his ear to the hole.

A long, blue snout, like a furry snake that had been driven over, shot out of the hole and ripped off the top of his ear. In complete surprise and disgust, Wayland straightened and took three hurried steps away from the burrow, clutching his ear and screaming loudly. His foot thumped into a rock as he moved, tripping him head first into the mud pool.

A loud scream was cut off quickly as he saw the hot mud coming towards his face. Wayland clamped his eyes and mouth shut tight just as his face impacted with the brown surface. There was a noise like a wet fart as his whole body splattered mud in all directions. With his mouth shut tight, Wayland was unable express the full terror of his emotions as the boiling mud oozed over his bare skin and began to penetrate his clothing. The heat was intense, stripping layers of skin, melting his features into amorphic lumps. The mud seeped into his nose, burning its way into his lungs, dragging the very life from his body. His entire form was on fire now as he sunk deeper. His life flashed before his eyes, he tried to look away, ashamed at how short the display was. The mud flowed over his head, igniting the …

Actually, it wasn't. Although it was hot, it was no hotter

than his fortnightly bath. True, the mud was going up his nose and drowning him, but the heat was supplied mostly by his imagination. Right, so I don't burn to death, I drown, thought Wayland as his outstretched arms touched the bottom.

Wayland turned around and sat up, gasping lung fulls of odorous, but welcome, air. What a prat, he thought, I was expecting it to be very hot and very deep. Of course it was neither, here at least. The hot mud bubbled around his chest as he sat contemplating his next move. The thick ooze had covered him entirely, leaving just two eyes staring out of a chocolate coloured lump. The heat from the mud was starting to relax him. It really was quite nice if you ignored the brown stuff.

He turned around and moved a little towards the beach, then laid back into the pool until his head touched the bottom with just his face out in the open. With one hand he scraped a relatively clear patch around his mouth and nose, then settled down for a good snooze.

Some hours later, he was awakened by an itching on his face. The mud had set out in the open, leaving a thick mask of brown. Laboriously, he climbed to his feet and waded out of the pool. More of the mud had stuck to his clothing, and on his bare skin. Wayland felt like he was walking around in a brown space suit. Now of course he had the problem of washing the stuff off, which of course didn't occur to him before. Wayland wondered if he could get back to his pool, that would be the ideal place. But he had no idea where that was, perhaps he could find another one.

He waddled up the beach like a penguin, dripping gobs of mud as he went. Carefully avoiding the burrows he continued along the sandbank looking for a place to climb up. Where the sandbank met the higher ground he had stumbled from earlier, the soil had crumbled away leaving a path even a man who looked like he'd terminally crapped himself could walk up. One foot in front of the other, Wayland made his way back into the jungle.

Warily, he crept between the trees, one eye open for the lobster-bug. Several minutes later, when nothing had happened, Wayland began to move more casually. Anyway, he thought, I don't think even that thing was hungry enough to eat me looking like this. That syndrome, known as commentators' curse, immediately came into action, proving his last words false.

Out of the jungle, mouth agape, not more than a couple of metres away, the lobster-bug appeared, running like the clappers on short legs straight at Wayland's face. He tried to turn, he tried to run, he wanted desperately to climb a tree, but the mud was drying fast making any of those actions very unlikely. So, he did the only thing left open to him, he screamed like a girlie.

The sound was muffled somewhat by the lack of jaw movement and a plug of mud on his upper lip, so it sounded more like a war cry than a full blown scream, but deep in his heart, Wayland knew he was going to die a wussy.

The strange head of the lobster-bug loomed nearer, he was able to count its pin sharp teeth, smell the slightly eggy odour of its breath, see himself reflected a thousand times in the multi-faceted eyes. He had to admit, he'd looked better. That time he'd woken up in a pool of his own vomit, wearing a sheet of bubble-wrap and thigh length waders filled with urine, then he'd looked worse, but that was the only time he could think of.

A blur of motion to his left caught his attention. The lobster-bug squeaked in a very high-pitched way then stopped moving. A sheen of sweat broke out on the creatures forehead as its eyes continued to move, but the rest of its body had frozen. A figure stepped from around the bug, dressed in full jungle camouflage.

"Ah, Wayland, there you are my boy." Said Sergeant Pettybone casually, as though they had met in the street. Behind him the two tank-like robots closely followed by Lionel emerged from the jungle.

"Thnkyoo srgunt." Wayland said through the now hardened mud mask. "Yr tinin is stot on."

"Ah, no trouble at all, now let's get you back to camp

and clean you up. Where the hell have you been? Everyone's going crazy trying to find you. Never mind, tell me later, I can see you're a little indisposed at the moment." Pettybone said helpfully, then lifted Wayland bodily and sat him on top of one of the robots. Wayland was elated, not only had he been rescued, but it seemed everyone had missed him and had actually been worried! That was nearly a dozen people who liked him now, an all time record.

As he sat grinning underneath the mud, he saw Pettybone walk over to the lobster-bug and pull two small objects from its flesh. The bug, now re-mobilised, rushed off in terror into the greenery. Pettybone replaced the objects into his top pocket, but pulled them out again when he saw Wayland looking. He held up two cocktail sticks. "One in the thick mass of the jaw bone and one in the upper front shoulder where it emerges from the shell, sets up a nerve block to the lower ganglions. Simple but effective, a trick I learned from an old hunter friend of my fathers. He used to take me to the park to play. If I could get past his hunting dogs without getting mauled he would buy me an ice cream. Nice bloke, got killed by a Yorkshire terrier. Someone threw it at his windscreen, smashed it to pieces, carried on through and lodged in his mouth. He choked to death on its collar trying to bite it in half. What a tragic waste. Still we inherited a fortune from him, which was nice. My dad built us a bomb shelter with it." Pettybone carried on for sometime, taking Wayland's silence for interest. Lionel and Wayland exchanged meaningful glances on several occasions.

The journey through the jungle finally ended by a long shingle riverbank, where a low, very modern looking shuttle waited for them. Sonia leapt from an open doorway as the party came into view. She stopped suddenly when she saw Wayland, then walked forward more cautiously when she realised he wasn't dead.

"Wayland, what happened to you? Where did you disappear to? We've had search drones and people looking everywhere, we thought you were gone. Then one of the scout droids picked up a signal not long back, we all scrambled but the signal disappeared before we got to you.

We thought we'd lost you forever." A small tear appeared in her eye, Wayland was touched, he didn't think anyone had ever shed a tear for him before. Except Marlo of course, when he had accidently spilled extra-hot chilli-pepper sauce down his y-fronts.

"Then the droid found you again and..." Sonia choked with emotion and tried to swallow the lump in her throat. Even encased as he was in muddy Y-fronts, Mr Stiffy found that amusing.

Quietly and with one hand on Wayland's encrusted shoulder, Sonia walked with the party to the shuttle and made sure he was loaded safely on board. The trip back was fairly subdued, with everyone wanting to know what had happened to him. He in turn was wondering how they had found him, and when, if ever, they were going to notice he was wearing a mud plaster cast and get him the hell out of it. It was starting to itch like mad now, he would have done anything to be able to scratch his balls.

The sensor vines on the flora station roof pulled back as the shuttle landed its cargo. The whole team were there to meet him, even Sean was grinning widely. Doctor Crippen had a large wheelchair with her, she was obviously eager to get her hands on him.

He was wheeled ceremoniously down to the surgery, the rest of the crew firing non-stop questions at him and Pettybone. At the surgery door Dr Crippen calmed everybody down in a professional manner, pushed him into the infirmary and closed the door, with all but herself and Lionel out in the corridor.

Lionel helped Wayland to stand, then into a shower cubicle. Lionel turned on the water, set the temperature to hand warm, then smiling, he left. Wayland heard them talking across the room, but couldn't hear what they were saying.

Slowly he rubbed his hands under the shower, peeling off the caked on mud. The water soon ran brown as the stuff began to loosen and fall. It came off in long strips and clumps as he worked at it, leaving the skin underneath clean and pink. When his hands were free he started on his face, easing his fingers under the mask and pulling it away in one go. It was such a relief when the mud peeled off, he scrubbed at his face, feeling the water wash him clean. As he washed he noticed the scar on his cheek was sensitive, tingling with the splashes of water. He probed the scar with his fingers and found the scar practically gone.

Quickly, or as quick as he could, he bent down and grabbed the rapidly dissolving mask. Sure enough, stuck to the inside of the mud pack was a propeller shaped piece of scar tissue. Wayland stopped himself calling out just in time. On second thoughts he thought, I'll keep this to myself for the moment. He threw the mask back down and squashed it with his foot. Then he remembered his ear, which had been bitten off by that snakey thing. It too was itching and had already begun to grow back. Well, well, he thought, healing mud, I could make a fortune with that.

Later, when he'd finally de-mudded himself, changed his clothes, been through the question and answer session and finally been left alone, he went over the events of the last month and the things that had happened. Purposefully, he hadn't told anyone all the details, especially about Honee. Some of the things he had discovered could be worth a lot of money to the right people, and he wanted to be one of them.

The next morning, Dr Crippen announced that Wayland would have to go back to the hospital at headquarters to be tested for parasites and internal injuries or malnutrition. She argued that she didn't have the proper expertise or equipment to carry out the tests herself. To Wayland's surprise, several of the crew, and especially Sonia, complained loudly when they heard. But the doctor was insistent, and everyone saw the sense of it in the end, if it was for Wayland's own good.

So, another noisy procession formed as this time Wayland walked out to a waiting shuttle. Shouted goodbyes and jovial banter echoed along the corridor and in through the craft's hatch, almost non-stop, until the door closed and he was air-lifted away. The crew were very respectful and attentive, asking him questions about his visit to the wilds.

Apparently he had become quite a celebrity on the news hungry colony.

After a largely uneventful flight, the shuttle landed on the hospital roof where a team of medics waited with a wheelchair. The shuttle door was slid open and the medics soon had him loaded in the chair, despite his protestations of being perfectly able to walk. An orderly procession then formed, pushing Wayland into a large lift, down a short corridor and into a private room. Wayland was impressed, the room was almost as large as a ward on one of the lower floors, with every bedside gadget he could want, all remotely controlled. It was tastefully decorated in shades of pink and yellow, with green curtains and carpets. The obligatory painting, which looked like it had been rendered by the interior designer's dog, on acid, was bolted to the far wall. A door he had been told led to an en-suite bathroom stood closed near the main door. He wasn't quite sure what an on-sweet was, but no doubt he'd find out later. Briefly he wondered who was paying for all this, he knew it wasn't him because he was skint. The thought faded as a passing female doctor winked at him.

At last, the medics left leaving one nurse behind who showed how all the controls worked, and with a final smile, the nurse left him alone. He had been sat on the bed and the wheelchair was folded up not far away. He had a feeling he would be needing it again when they began to probe his nether regions with all manner of tubes and bits of wire. Having your rectum examined tended to make you walk funny.

A look of complete horror clamped itself on his face, "What if they can tell I've been butt-fucked? I'll be the laughing stock of the colony." He said aloud, hands to his face. Talking to himself was a habit he had started out in the jungle and something he had not yet managed to control. I've got to get out of here, he thought, in case someone notices.

Before he had chance to think about an escape plan the door opened and in walked a nurse. To Wayland's disgust the nurse was a man. He was about one metre eighty tall, had very short brown hair and grey eyes. He was wearing a white one piece overall with a name badge which read, 'F. Nightingale, nurse.'

"Hello, Mr Snowball, my name's Fulton. I'll be your nurse for this evening. You've missed breakfast I'm afraid, but dinner will be served at twelve, so at least there's that to look forward to. You'll find meal times are the highlights of your day in this place. Except for your arrival this hospital hasn't seen so much activity since that dose of resistant crab-lice went through the junior doctors two years ago. If you need anything just ring, it's that red button there," He waved his hand generally in the direction of the panel on the wall behind the bed. "You can undress if you like, or wait 'til later, it doesn't bother me either way. I'll nip back later, meanwhile there's a lady porter two floors down who's gagging for it." With a sly grin he turned and walked out, rather quickly. My kind of guy, Wayland thought, brightening, perhaps it won't be so boring after all.

His small case had been brought in with him, so he got off the bed and unpacked his few belongings into a cupboard. There was already several garments in there, mostly immaculately clean and pressed pyjamas and two or three dressing gowns in a man's dark blue. We know where they'll be going when I leave thought Wayland. Under the tilt-and-swivel bed he discovered a pair of real leather moccasins. Great! He thought, man's slippers. Deciding he could get used to this, and wanting to make the most of it, he undressed, put on the pin-stripe pyjamas and walked over to check out the on-sweet doofa.

It turned out that en-suite was just a posh word for a private toilet, in which he was delighted to find a bidet. It brought back memories of a girl he used to know who insisted on rushing to the bidet when he had got his rocks off, to wash herself out. He sat on the edge of the plastic bum-basin for sometime wondering what had happened to odd-tits O'Grady, as they used to call her, not very kindly he now thought. Her left one was a handful and the right two, otherwise she was a nice girl, voice like a ref's whistle. He'd borrowed money off her lots of times, he supposed he ought to pay it back one of these days. She'd taught him a lot though, being three years older, mainly about sex and pizza, and how the two went together. The relationship didn't last of course, when a man is only seventeen three nights is a long time. But they didn't waste any time getting over each other, in fact the bidet was used twice on the third night, the second time after he'd walked out with her best friend, Gengisella.

His reverie was disturbed by the opening of the outer door.

"Mister Snowball?" A soft voice called.

Wayland got up and walked out of the bathroom. In the main room, half in, half out the door, stood a small, thin man wearing a white coat and a stethoscope. A long thermometer protruded from his top pocket, alongside an otoscope. Wayland's sharp eye and razor wit immediately labelled him a doctor.

"Yes," said Wayland simply.

"Ah, there you are. My name is Doctor Pecker, I have been assigned to you. If you could just lay on the bed for me and I'll give you a preliminary examination. Basically, this means taking you're blood pressure, making sure your eyes are clear and your ears too, asking some important questions about diet and bowel movement, which may at first seem irrelevant, or even intrusive, but I assure you the answers you give will be very useful and of course fully confidential, O.K?"

"Er, yes, I suppose so," Wayland answered unsurely.

The doctor had already wrapped a plastic thing around his arm, without waiting for an answer, which began to inflate by itself. "Right. Have you been feeling dizzy or weak?"

"No."

"Any headaches or impaired vision?" Dr Pecker held the stethoscope to Wayland's chest.

Wayland thought eyes always came in pairs, but as the answers the doctor expected looked to be 'no' he answered "No."

"Any panic attacks, feelings of rejection or inadequacy?" said the doc, pushing a silver torch thing into his ears.

"No."

"Any strange movements under your skin or in your bowels?" Dr Pecker looked right into his eyes, holding up the eyelids and squinting into the corners. His breath smelt of tuna and spring rolls.

"No!"

"And when was the last time you had a good crap?"

"No."

"Sorry?"

"Sorry, I mean, yesterday, just after breakfast."

"You didn't save it did you?" The doctor said hopefully.

"Er, no I didn't, does it matter?"

"No, it's fine, we'll just have to wait for another one. You'd be amazed what we can tell from a good stool sample, all sorts of things crawling around in there. Next time you go, catch it in one of those bowls in the toilet. Otherwise I think you are remarkably healthy, a fine specimen. All that outdoor living and low fat eating has done you good. You couldn't leave your body to science in your will could you? It would mean a lot to me if you did. Always short of decent cadavers, the ones we usually get are so wrecked they aren't much good. We had one in last week, uh, you should have seen it, liver all in bits, kidneys shot, pancreas in a right state, too much alcohol and not enough exercise, thoughtless bastards." The doctor fell silent for a few minutes. "Anyway, enough of my soapboxing, I'll see you again tomorrow, we will need to take you down for a full body scan, a few blood tests, won't take long. Then, if everything proves negative, you can go. Three, four days tops. O.K? Fine. See you."

Doctor Pecker turned swiftly and walked out of the door. A second later he came back, "Don't forget to catch your stool sample." He smiled brightly, then disappeared again.

Wayland was baffled, the entire visit had taken only a minute and a half, during which time the doctor had seemed to ask for his body and told him to peel bits off the furniture, whilst simultaneously forcing cold metal things into him.

Later, just after Wayland had discovered the porn channel on the wide-screen tele, a green liveried porter arrived with his dinner.

The porter lifted his round hat, revealing a bald patch in the centre of slightly greying hair and said, "Good afternoon to you young sir, may I say it is a pleasure and a privilege to serve a celebrity such as yourself. Today's repast is prawn cocktail, steak, served on a bed of chips and peas, and for sweet, a rather charming arrangement of fruits ensconced in raspberry ripple ice cream. Please enjoy your meal." The man, middle-aged, of average height and build but with sharp bluish-grey eyes, took exactly half a pace back and smiled warmly.

"Thank you. You, er, you always worked here then?"

"Indeed not sir, how astute of you to notice, I was once head waiter at the rather exclusive "\(" club, a fine gentlepersons retreat on the planet 'Etherweb.'"

Wayland ignored the ponsey shrimp thing and went straight for the steak and chips, between mouthfuls he asked the porter, whose name turned out to be Crawford X Todger-Johnson, how he had come to end up on this bog of a place.

"Alas sir, for reasons I favour not to disclose, I found cause to leave Etherweb with some alacrity. The first craft leaving that pleasant orb, as it transpired, was Greenshy bound, much to my chagrin. But, as the sages are oft heard to remark, mendicants are seldom allowed the extravagance of option. To my deepest woe it also came to pass that this was the only location I was able to acquire employment in the measly time span allotted me. So, my not inconsiderable proficiencies, learned at great expense, are squandered on petty duties the like of which one would normally delegate to a junior of lesser years." Crawford shook his head sadly.

Wayland had understood almost every other word of that, but he thought he had the gist of it. "Do you do any of that butlering as well? Only I've always wanted one, if I get rich you can come and work for me, be my girl friday and all that."

"Sir is very kind to offer such pulchritude on the basis of a woefully short acquaintance, were sir to inherit but a trifle from his elders I would be honoured to assist you in your daily duties."

"Er, yeah, great, I'll let you know." Wayland replied somewhat unsure of what he was answering.

"Now sir I am afraid I have others duties which demand my immediate proximity. I shall return." With a deep bow and a flourish, Crawford left the room, backwards.

"What a nice bloke," said Wayland, "Daft as a twat, but harmless enough."

Wayland watched the porn channel on his state-of-the-art, in your face, big screen tele, for a while, then had to go to the bathroom. As he was here anyway, he decided he needed a crap. The doctor's words finally sunk in about a sample, so toilet roll over face, he fished around for some before he flushed it. He had just captured a nice piece when he heard the sound of someone crying. He wrapped up his sample in the packaging thoughtfully supplied and stopped to listen. The sobbing seemed like it was coming from the room next door, probably a bathroom like his, judging by the slight echo. The sobbing turned into a wailing cry, then a screaming banshee wail counter-pointed by a rhythmic thumping. The wail gradually faded, but the thumping got louder and was now interspersed with choice four-letter words, and some longer ones. Wayland was well impressed, if you're going to throw a wobbler, that's the way to do it. Several lung bursting minutes later, after an almighty crash, the crying stopped. Wayland, with a glass pressed up against the wall, could hear a soft female voice offering words of comfort.

With the show over, and all of his toilet habits taken care of, he went back to bed and watched a film on the cheap repeats channel you get with every package. A light supper completed his rather hectic day, he laid down and fell quickly asleep.

Chapter Eleven

Prodded and Poked

"No!" Thump.

"Mumblemumble."

"No!" Bash.

"Mumblemumble."

"You fucking eat it then!" Crash!

At first Wayland thought it was another of his weird dreams, but as he slowly dragged himself back to what he considered awake, he realised the sound came from next door. The same room as the crying last night. Wayland leapt up, snatching a glass from the bedside table. There was nothing like a bit of live entertainment to cheer you up. Wayland pressed the glass to the wall and his ear to the glass. The only noise he could hear was someone sweeping up glass and the murmur of a calm male voice. Damn, he thought, missed it all. Of course it wasn't being nosy, someone might have been in trouble, it was only neighbourly to take an interest in these things.

The door swung open and Crawford walked in with a breakfast trolley. "Good morning sir, I have your breakfast for you. The selection is limited to half a dozen items but I think sir will find something to gratify his jaded palette." The porter seemed to completely ignore the fact of Wayland being practically stuck to the wall with a makeshift listening device in his hand.

"Great, thanks Crawford. Whose the witch in the room next door?" Wayland was never one for subtlety.

"Alas sir, a tragic accident, rendering the daughter of prominent politician Philip Udd marred for life. She being a fine girl on the very edge of the flight towards womanhood, cruelly brought down by the arrows of outrageous fortune."

"She's rich then?" Asked Wayland, not knowing his Shakespeare from his spokeshave.

"Indeed sir, or at least the paternal parent possesses certain available funds."

"Do you think she'd like to come round for breakfast?" Asked Wayland eagerly.

"Whilst I admire your optimistic approach, I fear however, a girl who resorts to almost decapitating the staff with a breakfast tray isn't suitable company for a man in your condition sir."

"Well, it was worth a try, if she's rich and ugly I thought I might be in with a chance, you know, because nobody else wants her."

"Your heart is clearly in the right place sir, But I would advise caution should your paths converge, her father is infamous for his removal of things he finds offensive, and is said to keep the removed objects in pickle jars in his study."

Wayland walked quickly over to the bed and got in, pulling the sheets tightly over his middle.

Crawford served him in bed, a mix of fried bacon, sausages, various other meats and eggs, full cream milk and orange juice. He didn't drink the juice. Breakfast over with, Dr Pecker returned, followed by Crawford and another porter, a young boy who looked about six, pushing a trolley.

Dr Pecker kept up a commentary all the way down to the scanning labs, telling Wayland what he was about to have done to him, and when he would be able to crap straight again. The two porters remained silent.

Many floors and several identical corridors later, the trolley finally came to rest in a long narrow room. At one end stood a flat, concave ledge with a thin blanket on it. He was quickly moved to the ledge, which seemed to float on nothing, then told to lie still.

"Now, Wayland, this scan with tell us many things, it will show us your bone structure, your nervous system, and the patterns of thought going through your head, among other things, the lymphatic system for one, but you probably won't understand that kind of thing so I won't mention it.

It's perfectly safe, so just lie still, don't move until we come back for you, and don't worry if things start to appear out of the wall, it's all part of the process. Now, it will take us a couple of minutes to get behind the lead wall on the other side of the car park, so don't worry if nothing seems to happen for a while, O.K? Good."

Wayland was left alone in the long room, only his thoughts for company, both were pretty lonely. He tried to lie still on the cold ledge, but some strange force made him twitch in anticipation. After four or five long minutes a light, somewhere behind him, began to flash. Then, one by one, hundreds of slender rods grew out of the wall, accompanied by a rising hum. The rods bloomed open at the end, saucer-shaped instruments forming an almost complete dome around him. The hum grew louder and higher until it went out of his hearing range, leaving a teeth rattling sub-noise behind.

For a long time nothing more happened. Wayland tried his best to lie perfectly still, but had to move to breathe, and one time to scratch his nuts. His patience, normally very good, was beginning to wear thin, his teeth itched and he was sure he could smell burning. The rods began to turn, some moved lower whilst others pulled back, forming a double-shelled half dome.

The noise stopped suddenly and all the rods folded back into whatever niches they came out of. Three minutes later Dr Pecker and two different porters, both woman and proud of it, came to collect him. "Well, Mr Snowball," began the doctor, the two woman laughed openly. "All seems to be in order, we'll know more when the full results come through, but it looks like you'll be able to leave in a day or two." Pecker smiled brightly, "And don't forget our little promise," he winked and tapped the side of his nose. "By the way, don't let anybody tease you, it looks perfectly all right, in fact I think it suits you. Bye!" With that cryptic remark the doctor slipped away.

Back in his room, Wayland stripped off and examined his entire body, well, he stood examining his meat and two veg for many minutes, and had a cursory look at the rest of his anatomy.

Finding nothing out of place, and starting to get a stiffy, he dressed quickly in normal clothes and decided to go for a walk.

A quick scout around and a fortuitous find of a visitor's map, he quickly located a roof top garden at one end of the towering 'L' shaped structure. The brochure said the building was one hundred storeys high and could house the entire population of the colony should it become necessary. It had been the first building constructed after planet fall; the backers had expected a lot of injuries and new diseases, estimating a profit of several million pounds through medical bills.

The garden turned out to be a bit of a disappointment, being just a collection of half dead plants growing in large containers. A group of gardeners were busy at one end flame-throwing native plants to keep their numbers down. He walked to the opposite end and found a sculptured bench; 'Man eats microwave lunch' it was called, according to a little plaque nailed to the base. It looked more like an accordion with a hard-on to Wayland, but he wasn't exactly an expert.

Nevertheless, he sat down, trying to get comfy on the hard surface. An overlooked sensor vine had got a foothold on the outside ledge and was sprawling along the roof behind the bench. Out of habit Wayland stretched out his hand, mentally asking the vine to come to him. The plant reacted almost immediately, its green stem rasping the ground as it slid towards him. The vine felt good under his hand, he sat running his fingers along the green skin, it reminded him of Honee, not the green bit, just the fact of where he met her.

"How did you do that?" A soft voice to his left said.

Wayland nearly jumped off the roof with fright. The sensor vine reared up between him and the voice, ready for any attack. Half of a young face peaked from behind the lumpy bit in the sculpture, a single eye looked at him moistly, "Sorry, I didn't mean to frighten you, I just wondered how you managed to make a plant move for you." The voice was soft, like a newly hatched duckling, thought

Wayland. It had a strange, distant sadness to it, remote and withdrawn.

"It's ok I didn't see you there, I thought I was alone. I'm Wayland, by the way, Wayland Snowball." He held out his hand. Without moving from her place, the girl reached out and softly shook his hand. It was warm, soft and just a little damp, like the skin at the top of your crack. "I come here sometimes to be alone, nobody else has found my hiding place yet, except for you of course." Although the girl was looking at Wayland, the voice seemed to be directed at someone else, someone a lot closer. Her sentences drifted off at the ends, fading to silence.

"Are you staying at the hospital, as a patient? Or do you work here?" asked Wayland politely. The vine had resumed its position in his hand, calmed by Wayland's settled emotions.

"Patient? Yes I suppose I am, though what they can do for me I don't know. Daddy, says they can fix it almost as good as new, but almost isn't quite the same is it? Everyone will know, they'll point and say 'oh, you can only tell if you look really close'. Bastards!" She suddenly yelled into the wind, startling Wayland again, causing the vine to pull back in fear.

After several minutes of silence the girl spoke again, this time normally. "Sorry, I get depressed, I've been very moody since the accident. I'm Robyn, I'm supposed to be in surgery, but I got scared and came up here to hide, they've been up twice to look for me, but they don't know about this little cave. What about you, brain surgery is it?"

"No, I was in the jungle for a month or so, they brought me in for tests, I think I've had most of them, I leave tomorrow." After a pause Wayland said "why did you think I was here for brain surgery?"

"Because of your hair, I thought they'd shaved your head to open it up." A hint of a smile could be seen on the side of her face that was visible. Wayland slapped his hands to his head. His hair was almost completely gone, just smooth skin left behind. "The bastards," he screamed emotionally. "They said it wouldn't hurt, wait 'til I see that little Pecker. I'll rip his hairs out one by one, then I'll start on the ones on his head." His fists gripped reflexively, anticipating the task.

"Actually, I think it quite suits you, you have a good build, quite muscular. Short hair always looks good on that sort of face." Robyn stopped suddenly, blushed a very becoming pink, then moved out of sight.

Wayland was stunned, women kept throwing themselves at him. Ever since he had gone astray in the jungle. Perhaps that's what people had meant when they told him to get lost? Slowly he moved over and leaned around to look into the hidden alcove. Eyes met and locked, brown and green. The girl screamed, "No, don't look, don't look at me!" and covered her face with her arms. A muffled sobbing began under the limb barricade.

Before her reaction, Wayland had got a quick look at the girl's whole face. One side was normal, actually quite cute, with deep, green eyes, reddish brown hair and a small nose. The right side was horrific, burned and scarred, like a wax bust melting in an old horror film. Her eye was all right, as was much of her nose, but from the top lip, up past her temple and back to her ear, the wound had bitten deep.

Wayland spoke softly, gently, "It's all right, I'm sorry I startled you. I didn't mean to pry, It's just that I'm not used to women saying nice things to me. Please, don't cry, just talk to me for a while."

"I don't believe you," she said, emerging slightly, "About women I mean, anyway, I'm not a woman, not yet, daddy says I'm just a girl."

"Of course you're a woman, how old are you, eighteen?" Actually she looked a lot older with that face, but he'd learned something about women in his twenty three years, even if it was only one thing. "Besides, dads always say that about their daughters, you're my little girl and all that."

Robyn lowered her arms to her knees, "Yes, I suppose they do, but I'm only seventeen, well, I'll be eighteen in a few months, so I suppose you are close enough. Now, I bet you want to know what happened?"

Wayland, who was dying to know, and trying not to stare, managed to keep a calm expression and say, not too casually, "If you want to tell me, I'll listen. Otherwise it's none of my business." The vine had crept back to his hand, he stroked it comfortingly.

"Well, I'll tell you, because each time I do it gets easier, less hurtful. My father, you may have heard of him, Philip Udd, the politician, but that's not his fault, somebody has to do it. Anyway, it so happens that a certain other, highly placed off world official is visiting this planet, looking for a possible investment. He brings with him his son, an oily, creepy little knob who takes after his father. So daddy says 'entertain sonny-boy, impress him anyway you can, see if you can get him to stay, I know he's a snotty little whip-dick, but don't forget who his father is.' Great, I think, all daddy wants me for is to use as a pawn in his political games. Anyway, we meet up outside my place, he picks me up, you know, lover-boy, in this flash private hover-thing and off we go into the sunset. After a few drinks he starts to get frisky, hands wandering like a policeman on a strip-search. Pack it in I say or you'll lose some fingers. Do you know what he says? I'll tell you. He says, 'my father told me you have to be nice to me or your father will regret it.' Well that was it, I stood up, grabbed the steak au pouivre and slammed it in his face. 'Bitch! He shouts, 'I'm going to tell my father on you.' Then, brain donor of the year picks up the brandy and throws it in my face, the whole glass full, and it, of course, being on fire." Robyn stopped talking and swallowed hard, then, somewhat unsteadily, she continued. "I turned my face in time to stop it going in my eyes, but I wasn't fast enough to stop this," She gestured towards her face. "The spirit had some other ingredients in it apparently, it stuck to my face and neck, splashed my arms and hands, my hair caught fire. You know what the little shit did? He ran away, panicking like a little sheep. It was left to the waiters to smother the fire with wet towels. I was rushed to hospital, where most of the damage, at least the surface burns, were taken care off. Look," She pulled back her sleeves. New, pink flesh encased her lower arms. She pulled the sleeve back quickly.

- 118 -

Robyn sighed, took a deep breath to calm her emotions, then continued. "The worst thing about all this was my dad's reaction, he said I was to blame, that I lead the boy on. Then he says no action will be taken, in fact it is not to be mentioned again. He had the brass nerve to bring the boy and his father into my hospital room. There I was hooked up to all these machines and they're talking about the weather and how nice the wallpaper is. I tell you, if I could have got up I would have shoved the son right up his smarmy daddy's arse." Robyn fumed quietly for a few moments, then when their eyes met again she smiled, "I've never told anybody that bit before." She laughed brightly, "Well, that conjures up all sorts of images in my head, I don't know about you?"

Wayland smiled, her laugh had conjured up images all right, he was wondering what the rest of her looked like, all pink and glistening. "I have very interesting thoughts in my head, yes."

He changed the subject. "How long have you been here?"

"In the hospital? Oh, weeks. It seems like years. My dad insists I'll never catch a good man looking like this, I suppose he's right, but the sort of man he wants me to catch is very different from the one I want."

"I think he's wrong. If a man is interested in you like that, then he can obviously see beyond the exterior, into the proper you. Beauty is in the soul as well as the skin." As soon as he'd said it, Wayland grimaced inside, where the hell had that bullshit come from? he thought. Three months ago he would have turned her over and shagged her from behind, so he couldn't see her face. Now he was spouting philosophy at her.

"Wayland? That was lovely, and do you know, you're right. I'm going to walk proudly, in public. I'll wear my scars as a symbol of all that is rotten and corrupt in our society. I'll make people look, and I'll say 'This is what you have done to me, you and your petty concerns.'" She took a breath to continue, Wayland quickly interrupted, the gobby cow will go on all night at this rate. "That's all well and gravy, but actually I have a better idea. I think I can help you get rid of it all together, the scar I mean."

"Oh, Wayland could you?" A woman's vanity was almost as strong as a man's jelly effect. She forgot almost immediately about any 'visual protests'. "Could you really cure me? I mean the doctors have all said it will take major reconstruction work to put me right, and then there would still be a join."

He moved closer, turning his cheek towards her. "I had a big, propeller shaped scar there, less than a week ago, and there." He showed her the nearly healed tip of his ear. "A snake thing bit my ear off, it started to grow back, but I think I need more treatment. If you look really close you can see it's still a bit pink, but the skin on my cheek is indistinguishable from the other one." Wow, that was a big word, what next? Wayland thought privately.

"You wouldn't be trying to kidnap me or anything would you? Daddy won't pay up, he's a tight bastard at the best of times."

"No, of course not. I swear to you I mean you no harm. I can't guarantee it will work, but it's worth a try isn't it?"

"Yes, I suppose so. What do I have to do? And if you say strip off I'll rip your nuts off, I can, my father hired me a special coach, I could rip your nuts off and make them into earrings, not that I'd want to, but I sure could." From the determined look on her face, Wayland didn't doubt her in the least, in fact he was so convinced he drew his knees in as tight as he could. "No, of course not. Listen, I've got a girlfriend all ready, she's very nice. She's away on business at the moment. You're quite safe with me."

Robyn examined Wayland for a moment then spoke, "Right, where do we go?"

"Well, do you have a shuttle or some kind of flying transport? We need to go quite a distance."

"Yes, daddy keeps a small business cruiser in the hanger near our quarters. I could borrow the key. But how far are we going? I thought most of the colony buildings were quite near."

"We aren't going to a building. Trust me, it's a surprise."

* * * *

Robyn didn't entirely trust Wayland, she had him checked out by her dad's data service, which found only the stuff about his trip through the jungle. She also procured a small but extremely debilitating triple beam pulsed laser blaster, which she slipped into a holster on her knickers. With the cruiser activation key nestled against her ample breast, she grabbed her bags and stealthily crept out into the night. The security systems, installed at great expense and guaranteed to detect all forms of intrusion, completely ignored her because she was going out, not coming in. The bodyguard assigned to her also failed to notice her departure, mainly because he was rogering the upstairs waiter on Mr Udd's specially imported blue baize snooker table.

They had agreed to meet on the corner of the road that ran beside the hospital, mainly because there was a small park there in which to hide. Wayland had been discharged, that phrase still made him laugh, despite his new found adulthood. He had said his goodbyes to Dr Pecker, who he didn't assault in the end, to Crawford and Fulton the nurse, and several other, female nurses he couldn't remember the names of but could still feel the warm patches their breasts had left on his chest as they kissed him goodbye. He was expected to resume his post at the flora station, but had been given two weeks leave to do with as he pleased.

Several times he had also tried to contact Honee, but he always got her answering machine. Although he left several messages, she never called back. He was beginning to think she had just used him for sex. Women!

The night was cool and clear, as most nights were on Greenshy. The meeting and subsequent borrowing of the cruiser went without incident and the two were soon ready to go.

"Does this thing have a shower?" Asked Wayland casually, as they stumbled around in the darkened craft.

"Oh yes, it has all the things we could possibly need for a trip into the jungle." She smiled broadly, the melted side of her face crinkling into a disgusting lunar landscape.

"You've worked it out then? I wondered if you would, but you don't know where." Wayland's smiled slumped like an old women's belly when she takes off her corset. He didn't know where he was going either. Damn, he thought, I couldn't even find my way back to the cave from half a mile away. What a dick head. Now what was he going to tell her? She would think him a right moron. It was Robyn who saved him. "If you're trying to work out how to find the place at night, this cruiser has the latest navigation equipment. Eadrot, that's daddy's pilot, showed me how to fly it once. I think he wanted to get my knickers off, but he was too scared of daddy in the end."

She began pressing switches, which in turn lit up panels and started computers. A soft voice spoke, "Good Evening Miss Udd, you have a visitor with you I see, do you wish me to make him comfortable or to vaporise his ass?" The question was asked in an emotionless monotone. Robyn turned to Wayland, "I've customised the character parameters a little, she doesn't talk like that to daddy. No, Margaret, he's a friend, for the moment."

Wayland sat in the co-pilot seat and stared into a screen indicated by Robyn. A three dimensional map appeared. It showed their present position, a low hangar and several taller buildings. "Can this thing search for stuff, you know, like geographical features and shit?"

"Oh, yes. If you want it to find you a warm, sandy beach, or a cool, grassy knoll, no problem. Just ask it what you want to search for."

Wayland knew he had been lost somewhere in the mammary plains, but wasn't sure which direction he had gone in to find the mud pool. "Er, computer?" He said nervously. "Can you find a place in the mammary plains that has, like, steam coming out of it?"

"Is this the gas people call steam, which is actually water vapour, or the gas that is actually steam and therefore invisible to the human eye?" Margaret asked with a hint of smarmyness.

"Er, I didn't know there was a difference, it's sort of warm and white and it rises into the air in thick clouds."

"The presence of such an obvious indication will render the site relatively easy to find. For your information; if you were to observe a boiling kettle you would see a gap between the white water vapour and the spout of the kettle, this gap is actually the steam, a gas and therefore invisible, before it cools to vapour. If you require further information I would be glad to supply it." Lectured Margaret.

"Thanks Margaret, but just find this place for us, quick as you like." Robyn commanded.

"Get a grasp of your shires a minute girl, this ain't no road taxi. We'll be ready to go in just a jiffy."

A low vibration, almost unfelt, began somewhere in the cruiser. A few minutes later they were airborne and heading for the plains. The pair watched the lights dwindle into the distance, then disappear. Looking out of the cockpit, Wayland and Robyn peer into the darkness ahead, unable to make out a single feature. "I hope this ship knows where it's going." Wayland asked nervously. Before Robyn could reassure him, Margaret jumped in. "I've got more sensors than you've had hot dinners, boy, so sit back and enjoy the ride. And stop thinking that I'm part of the ship, there's me, in this little orange box, then there's the ship, the big hunk of metal and plastic around you. While I might be driving this thing, in total control may I add, the two of us are separate entities, so don't you forget it, soft-brain."

"Margaret, be nice to our guest, at least until I say otherwise." Robyn reprimanded.

"Nice computer, did you say you programmed it yourself?"

"No, not programmed, just tailored slightly."

Wayland wondered what kind of girl tailored a computer to be belligerent.

A couple of hours later, with Wayland dozing in the chair and Robyn thinking about buying a motor bike so she could wear a helmet, the computer spoke again. "All right boys and girls, stand by your beds, heat source at twelve o'clock. Mammary plains, south-east of the centre about ten clicks west of the eastern boundary. I'm getting sulphur, I'm getting argon, I'm getting that toothpastie-damp-towel-just-had-a-bath odour. It's hot, it's wet, it's very slightly earthy-minerally. The sort of smell one would expect when one has just been bonked senseless on a pile of fresh hay. Is this what you're looking for?" Margaret said very dramatically.

Robyn looked at Wayland and blushed a slight pink. "I really don't know where she gets it from, certainly not from me, someone else must have been fiddling with her." She smiled shyly, then looked away.

Wayland was wondering what kind of girl he'd got himself lost in the jungle with. There was more than meets the eye to this young lady.

The computer announced the arrival of the cruiser at their destination, but was unable to land. A picture of the surrounding terrain, enhanced by the computer, showed a pool of thick liquid surrounded by trees. Wayland was impressed, "That certainly looks like the place, how far away can you land, Margaret?"

"Oh, it's first name terms now is it? Who gave … "

"Margaret, answer the question." Robyn said impatiently.

"Well, if you want to scorch some undergrowth, right here. Otherwise it's about an hour and a half walking in this terrain and those shoes."

"Listen, Margaret, can you see a patch of vines, you know, those long sensor vines?"

"I am well aware of the vines you mean, I am … never mind. Yes I can see a mass of them all tangled around each, what about it?" The computer asked in a demanding tone.

"If they weren't there, could you land?" Asked Wayland.

"What the fu … "

"Margaret!" Robyn gasped.

"Sorry, but can you explain what this little weasel, sorry, this young gentleman, is going on about?"

Wayland looked at Robyn, "Trust me, just get this thing over the patch and open the side door."

Robyn suddenly remembered the behaviour of the vine on the hospital roof. "Margaret, move directly above those vines and be ready to land. When you're there open the side door. O.K?"

"Well, I think you're crazy, but what the hell, one or two less humans in the world can't be all bad. Complying."

The cruiser lurched to port, swung to starboard, then settled above the vines. The side door open with a slight pop. Wayland looked down into the night, now he was away from the enhanced image he couldn't see very much, but he knew they were down there. He relaxed himself and tried to imagine that he needed to land, absolutely must land. "They're moving Wayland!" Came Robyn's excited voice from the cockpit, "Not enough to land yet though". Again he relaxed thinking deep thoughts, if only he could land this thing he could get Robyn naked in the mud pool.

"Wayland! They've moved! Did you see that? They shot out of there faster than I thought they could move." Robyn laughed.

The cruiser began to descend, almost dropping Wayland out of the door. "Get you next time," a voice whispered above his head.

Robyn walked out of the cockpit, "Right Margaret, light it all up, we might as well get comfy until morning."

As the door slid shut in front of him Wayland began to think how nice it would be if the vines climbed over the ship, hid it from the air and let the vines get a little warmth. He was rewarded by the computer shrieking, "Get them off, they'll damage the structure, Mr Udd will disconnect me for this. I'll get you back, Empath." The last word was meant as an insult, but Wayland took it differently. It also made him think of Honee, he had wanted to bring her here first, but he was sure she would understand, besides, she hadn't contacted him, so she should expect these things. He turned around, away from the door.

Wayland gasped. The interior was now lit up like a Christmas tree. When they had arrived they had purposefully kept it dark to avoid detection. Now it was revealed, Wayland couldn't believe such luxury could be crammed into a simple shuttle. Every wall, the floor and the ceiling were carpeted with thick Axminster. The furniture was real wood, oak probably, thought Wayland who knew oak when he saw walnut. Hidden lights shone on the key features, a multi-speakered entertainment centre, a fully automated kitchen, a square seating area, a boardroom table, and at one end a simulated log fire. Wayland was gob-smacked, he would definitely be getting one of these. On the wall opposite the cockpit were two doors in matching wood.

"Toilet, bedroom." Robyn pointed to each door in turn when Wayland asked. "You don't mind sleeping on the settee do you? There's only one bed, it's very big but … "She left the statement hanging, which was more than could be said for Mr Stiffy, who'd leapt up when Robyn had said bedroom in that sexy, come-get-me way. "Yes," He shouted, "I do mind, I want to sleep with you and bury my head in your tight fanny."

"It's ok I don't mind sleeping on the settee." Said Wayland, quite casually.

"What! Yes you do, go for the minge you spineless scrote-slayer." Mr Stiffy screamed.

"It looks very comfortable. Why don't we get some sleep now, and I'll take you from behin … from, er, I'll take you down to the treatment area when it gets light." Wayland smiled tightly.

Robyn smiled back, "All right, but I'm starting to get a good idea of what to expect, goodnight."

Wayland made himself comfy on the soft suite. It swallowed him into its fluffy cushions, warming and relaxing him. His mind was racing, Honee, he thought, Keep my mind on Honee, Honee. Be faithful to Honee. He fell asleep, thinking Honee. He dreamed of honey, dripped over Robyn and licked off.

Chapter Twelve

Makin' Bacon

The next morning, after a long English breakfast and a quick shower, cold in Wayland's case, they dressed in the spare clothes they'd bought, more suitable for jungle walking and something washable. Robyn was very excited now, her burned skin crinkling almost audibly as she chattered away. "You are sure this is going to work aren't you? I mean it worked for you, so why shouldn't it work for me?" She gushed.

"Well, I didn't promise it would, but yes, it worked a treat for me. I hope you're prepared for a surprise, and don't worry how it looks, it will all be worth it in the end." said Wayland.

"I think I know what to expect, that's why we're wearing clothes that can be rinsed out. And all that talk of steam between you and Margaret. It's a hot spa pool isn't it? A natural hot water spring with healing properties. Isn't that wonderful?" Robyn hopped through the jungle, full of life and energy. Wayland was proud it was he who was responsible for her new found cheerfulness.

"You're not quite right, but you're very near." Wayland edged.

The cloud of steam was thick today, as only a light breeze disturbed it. They had only to walk a few metres to the shingle beach Wayland had found before.

"Robyn, let me go first, There's a long beach along this way, and there are also a few large animals around. When we get to the beach, stay away from the tunnels in the bank."

Wayland was in control today, he wasn't afraid of the big lobster bugs, or the furry snakes. Being lost in the jungle had taught him many things, one of which was to carry a five beam, continuous burn slicing laser, like the one he had found in the cockpit and which was now in his pocket.

He led the way towards the end of the beach where the caved in section could be traversed. The crunch of gravel under heavy boots soon told him they'd arrived.

"Phew, that does smell a little peculiar doesn't it? And what's that strange bubbling noise? There aren't any creatures living in this spa are there?" Robyn asked rather nervously.

"No, nothing at all in the, er, no not that I've seen." Wayland mumbled, he wasn't sure how a girl from her background would take mud-bathing. He soon found out.

"Yuck, the water is all brown, Wayland, what's happened to it?" Robyn screwed up her face, making the average moon look like a billiard ball in comparison

"Actually Robyn, it's mud," Wayland said somewhat sharply. "If you want your face healed you will have to wear some of that, and if you've got burns elsewhere, you'll have to bathe in it too."

Robyn's mouth dropped open, she looked at the mud, then at Wayland, then back at the mud, then she spoke, very determinedly. "Right, you first."

"Right, no problem, it's a bit hot when you first get in, but after that it's really relaxing."

Before he could stop himself, he had stripped naked and began to wade slowly into the hot mud. He was almost up to his genitals when he remembered he was with Robyn, not Honee. Slowly he turned around to look at her. She was standing stock still on the bank, her mouth slightly open, her head turned away but her eyes looking at his manhood, her face the colour of the inside of a woman's love tunnel.

"Sorry, shall I …? No, I'll just go in." Wayland waded in deep and sat down, hiding his body up to the neck. Robyn stood where she was for a while, then loosened her clothing and began applying the thick mud to her scar. When she'd put enough on she glanced at Wayland, then looked away. "What now?" She asked rather shortly.

"Oh, just let in dry for a while, it peels off when it's set, hopefully taking the scar with it. I think my scar was quite shallow, so it came off with one go, it might take longer with yours. How long do you think we've got, I mean before your dad comes looking for us?"

"Oh, I left him a note saying I'd be back in a few days. I didn't mention you, I don't think he'd like you."

"Oh." Said Wayland simply, which was easy enough for him.

Wayland relaxed in the hot mud, thinking nice thoughts, about what he was going to do to Honee if, no when, she returned. Then he thought about a man's other love, beer. He wondered what it would be like to own a brewery. Before, he had dreamed of finding a girl whose father owned a pub, now he realised he was aiming too low. Might as well go for the entire plant. Imagine all those vats of beer, megalitres of the stuff, enough to swim in! Sip, stroke, sip, stroke, right across the pool.

A squeal brought him staggering to his feet, his half erect, mud covered dick pointing straight at Robyn. She didn't seem to notice. She was too busy staring at a face-shaped piece of mud clutched in her hand. "Look, Wayland! Look! It's coming off!"

Robyn ran over to him, slopping up to her knees in mud. "Look, you can already see bits of skin flaking away. What does it look like? Is it healing? Please tell me it's healing."

Wayland looked closely, it was a mess, worse than before. Her scar tissue had begun to melt and run into one big glacier of ugliness. "Yes, it certainly looks better, healing nicely I'd say. Of course I'm no expert, but I think a few more applications should do it." He lied casually.

"Wow, this stuff is great. If you weren't covered in it I'd kiss you. Right, I'm going to put some more on." Robyn waded a few metres away and began to apply more mud, this time thicker and with more confidence. Wayland laid back down, leaned so his ear was in the mud and carried on with his daydream.

Several hours of daydream later, men can concentrate really well sometimes, Wayland's ear began to itch annoyingly. Right, he thought, that's enough for today. He stood, flaking off the layer of mud that had dried on his front. The rest he left on to dry. Robyn was sitting on the beach, her bare feet in the hot mud. She had applied two lots now, allowed it to dry, peeled it off and was starting on her third. Wayland smiled down at her, "Are you ready to go now? Put a good thick layer on and we'll go back to the cruiser. It works better if it dries completely." Wayland was hoping this was the case, he would hate to have brought her here for nothing. There was no way she was going to let him in her knickers if this stuff didn't work. Then again would he want to?

"My face is tingling, is that usual?" She asked somewhat worriedly.

"Oh yes, that means it's working." Actually, he wasn't sure, but his face seemed to itch when he put it on. It would be terrible if she peeled off the mud and her face came with it. Leaving just a skull and the side of her mouth, her teeth grinning through the gap. He shook his head, what a sick thought.

Robyn stood slowly, looking at Wayland's crotch. At first he though his luck was in, until he looked down. The mud around his half-erection had set in that shape, leaving him looking like a chocolate banana. Hastily, he turned away and grabbed at his mud knob. To his horror it broke off in his hand. Wayland stood very still for several minutes, not daring to look down. Side effects, he hadn't thought of those. What if it makes the skin brittle after prolonged exposure? Robyn began to move around behind him, her feet crunching on the shingles. "Wayland? What's the matter? If you're embarrassed, don't be, I know all about men and what happens to their willies. I know you can't help it, I suppose I should be flattered. Come on, let's go back to the ship, here, I'll take your clothes. She turned away and walked slowly back towards the cruiser.

Wayland finally plucked up the courage to look inside the mud casting. To his immense relief, it was empty. Looking further down revealed a bare, mostly pink patch and a shrivelled dick. So all right, the mud had taken off his pubic hair, but hell, it could have been worse, much worse. He counted his testicles, checked his knob again, found everything in order, apart from several hundred missing short and curlies, then raced off to catch up with Robyn.

They took it in turns to shower off the mud when it had dried. Wayland, waiting in the other room, was expecting a scream any minute, so when Robyn emerged smiling, he was very relieved.

"It is working, I can feel it tingling, and it seems much smoother, not so cratered. I think a few more days here will do it. If it does take longer, are you all right to stay too? If you need to call anyone, I'm sure Margaret can help."

"No, it's fine. I mean there is someone, a friend really, but she's away on business. I can catch up with her whenever we return." He tried to sound casual, trying to sound like someone who had friends, not a sad git who wasn't needed anywhere. "I'm not expected back to work for another ten days, so no problem there."

"Where do you work?" Robyn asked, seating herself on the other end of the settee to Wayland.

"Oh, I work for the department of alien flora testing." He carefully didn't say 'as a general dogsbody.'

Robyn looked at Wayland in the way Honee sometimes did, no not that way, as though she was surprised. "You have hidden depths to you Wayland Snowball. You have a happy-go-lucky exterior, but underneath the skin you are a very caring, and intelligent man."

Wayland blushed to his hair roots, those on his head of course. "Er, thanks, you're not so bad yourself." He mumbled in reply.

Robyn stood up and moved closer. Mr Stiffy, fooled by the last few false alarms, sat still until he was sure he was going to be needed. Wayland thought she was going to stand in front of him, slowly undo her dressing gown, revealing a low cut basque, stockings and suspenders, crotchless, edible knickers, knee length leather stiletto boots and a jug of strawberry custard. Ah! The wonders of a man's vivid imagination! Not surprisingly, he was completely wrong.

Robyn leaned over and kissed him very sisterly on the forehead. "Thank you Wayland, for bringing me here, for giving me hope, and dragging me out of my blue funk. Goodnight, see you bright and early tomorrow." She smiled warmly, turned and headed for the bedroom. At the door she turned, "You will be alright on the sofa, won't you? I don't want you to think I'm hogging the bed."

"Oh no, no problem, this is very comfortable." Wayland smiled reassuringly. He was telling the truth, it was a very nice sofa, just a little lonely without Ro ... Honee.

When she'd closed the door behind her, Wayland tried to think back to their meeting, he could recall their conversation and movements completely, something he had been able to do recently, but couldn't recall touching or going anywhere near her blue funk. He didn't even know she owned a car.

* * * *

The next morning came, as mornings do, quietly and with much less fuss than a woman. Wayland was up and about half an hour before Robyn, a habit that still lingered from his jungle days, as he termed them. When she finally emerged she was smiling broadly, her face not crinkling half as alarmingly as before. Wayland beamed, she really was starting to look attractive. "Good morning Miss Udd, I trust you slept well?" He enquired politely.

"Yes, thank you, sir Snowball. Although my face was tingling I slept like a cut up tree. I think I must be catching up with all the sleep I missed after this happened." Robyn replied cheerfully, not even a hint of sadness with the mention of her scar. She also seemed to move more surely, as though she had decided something. Also, Wayland noticed, her dressing gown wasn't fastened up to her neck as usual, but hung open almost to her cleavage. Wayland interpreted this as meaning only one thing, she was gagging for it.

Trying to keep his mind on other things, Wayland asked her if she would like breakfast.

"Yes please, I have such an appetite, I could eat a horse between two bread vans. I think it's all this fresh air."

"I know what you mean. Tuck in, that autokitchen is really good, I think some of the food is real."

Whilst Wayland tried to work out why anyone would put bread in a van, Robyn wondered what other kinds of food there were. After a pleasant, unhurried repast, the two grabbed a picnic lunch, some clean towels and a few other essentials, and wandered over to the steaming mud pool.

To Wayland's great delight and surprise, Robyn began to strip off when they arrived. She spread out a thick towel on the shingles, then began removing her clothes. Wayland did the same, a bit slower this time. Without staring too much, Wayland watched as one by one, her garments were peeled away. Wayland groaned almost audibly when a yellow bikini was revealed. At this level, Robyn stopped disrobing and waded slowly into the mud. Carefully she sat down, then laid back, her head just short of the beach. Her mud covered hands came out of the water and she smoothed a thick coating of the healing ooze over her face.

"Wow," She exclaimed after a few minutes, "this is so relaxing, I could lay here all day. It clears the mind wonderfully, it's been a long time since I daydreamed." She lapsed into silence again.

For the rest of the morning the pair just rolled about in the mud, thinking, exchanging small talk, generally relaxing. The familiar tingling sensation turned to a faint itch, then, on Wayland's ear at least, it faded to nothing. "I think I might be done, my ear feels like it used to, and it's stopped itching."

Robyn sat up and leaned closer, studying Wayland's ears. Her warm breath felt good on his face, her body, steaming from the mud, felt even better as she rubbed against him. "Yes, they both look the same now, identical, no pink skin or anything. This mud is really good. You know, you could make a fortune bringing people here, or even taking the mud to them."

"No, I couldn't do that, not take it away, this place is special, you know, fragile. I don't want to ruin it." Robyn looked at him in that way again, "You really do like this place don't you? This planet I mean. With those vines of yours and this mud pool. You're the first person I've met who could really look at what this colony has to offer instead of complaining all the time. You could go far in this place, I'm sure of it." She smiled warmly and laid back in the mud.

Wayland had considered making money from this place, but the more he thought about it the less he liked the idea. He had now decided to keep this place a secret as long as he could, and the cave he had lived in. He wondered if he could buy the land, perhaps the whole of the mammary plains. No, what was he thinking? Any day now the Wayland curse would set in and he'd be back with Marlo, counting female condoms.

The next morning Wayland and Robyn repeated the actions of yesterday. Robyn's face was very smooth now, but still pink. Wayland thought she looked very attractive, almost too good to resist, but she had shown no sign of being attracted to him, and of course there was … er … Honee, there was Honee to consider.

So it came as a great surprise to Wayland, when, just after their picnic lunch, Robyn turned to Wayland and said, "Would you like to make love to me?" In a rather shaky voice. At first Wayland thought it was a trick question, never having heard it before. He tried to think of the right answer, but could only come up with "Yes."

Robyn rolled closer to him on the towels they had spread out. Their muddy bodies touched, then pressed together with a squelch. Wayland fumbled along her slippery back until he found the bikini straps. They had been tied rather tightly, so Wayland just pulled it up, sliding his hand over her breast. The nipple went hard under his hand, making Robyn gasp. She pulled her lips from his and leaned back slightly. Then she said the words a man loves to hear, "Wayland, I'm a virgin."

Wayland smiled tenderly, "It's ok so am I."

Her eyes widened, then seeing him smile she laughed. "I'm glad you're not, we could be here all day."

"That's not a problem. Relax, trust me." Their lips met again, the warm mud smearing over their faces. Robyn's bikini bottoms slid off down her mud covered legs, the top ended up forgotten around her neck. Wayland was already naked, but so covered in mud he had to wash off his hard-on with the bottled water they'd brought. Wayland slid his hand down over Robyn's belly and over her mound. "I see you've had the same problem with the pubic hairs." He whispered as he nibbled her ear.

"Yes, it all fell out in the shower last night, there's not a hair on my body, but my head hair is fine." Robyn giggled shyly. Wayland thought what a shame it was that all this mud was around, he'd love to lick her hairless fanny; maybe later.

His fingers found her wet hole, he slid them in as far as they would go, then pulled them out and began to rub around her clity. Robyn moaned softly, then louder as he increased the speed. When she was good and wet, and slippy with mud, he rolled onto her and slipped his dick in. She moaned with pleasure, "Oh, Wayland, I never thought it could be like this." Within minutes she was writhing around, loudly orgasming. Wayland hoped there was no one around, at least not within a kilometre, which was probably as far as she could be heard. The sight and sound of orgasm, plus the fact he hadn't had any in days made Wayland come, shooting his warm load right into her.

Then he wondered about precautions.

It turned out Robyn was fully covered in that department, thanks to her dad, who didn't want his precious darling ruining her body through childbirth. Paradoxically, he had also promised to castrate any man that got too close to her, with a seven-beam laser welder.

So, for the next few days they bonked like rabbits on fast forward; in the shower, on the settee, in the mud like two rutting pigs, in the cockpit with Margaret shut off, in the mud again, because they particularly liked that bit, and several metres in the air in a web of vines. Wayland got his wish to lick Robyn's smooth ginny, in fact there wasn't a lot on either of them that didn't get sucked or fucked one way or another. On the evening of the sixth day they realised they had had sex everywhere except in bed. So they went to bed.

On the morning of the seventh day, after a careful examination of each other's healed flesh, which turned into a rather close examination of each other's genitals, they decided that the mud had done its stuff. Robyn did indeed look very nice, now that both sides of her face were equal. The scar tissue had disappeared completely, leaving skin almost an exact match to the surrounding area. Wayland's ear was totally healed, so that not even a close examination showed up which one had actually been damaged. Robyn went into the cockpit, that word would forever bring a smile to her face, and asked Margaret to take them back to Pity.

Wayland stayed in the main seating area for a while, trying to work out what to say to her. He felt really bad about being unfaithful to Honee, and he wanted to get back to her. But how could he tell Robyn that he had someone else? After all they'd been through, and he had popped her cherry. Let her down easy, he thought, when we land just say "It's been nice knowing you, but I have some business to attend to. Goodbye, see you around." Then just walk away, easy as that. He smiled, his plan all worked out.

The journey back was uneventful, they were too exhausted, and too tense to even use the bed one more time. Instead they tidied up, or rather Robyn did, whilst Wayland switched off the autokitchen. In the darkness of night, they both thought it sensible to sneak back in, or as they put it, land with the minimum of fuss.

Margaret brought the cruiser to a perfect landing, softly and with little noise, inside the private Udd hanger. The door slid open on a breath of air, "Thank you for flying with shag-air, please come again." Said Margaret, in a husky, slightly mocking tone.

"You weren't supposed to be looking, you electronic voyager." Hissed Wayland angrily.

"You didn't say anything about listening." She retorted cheekily.

Wayland turned to find Robyn's green eyes staring back at him, a single tear sat on her cheek like a crystal bead.

"Goodbye Wayland, I had a really good time. Thanks for getting my face healed, I'll never forget you. If you like I could get my father to send you some money, or something. Perhaps I'll see you around." Robyn leaned over and kissed Wayland on the lips, then turned to walk down the ramp that had appeared beside the open door. Robyn's shape melted into the shadows that hung everywhere in the darkened hanger.

His mouth dropped open, "But ... " He began, aloud, that's my line, his thoughts continued. Dejectedly, Wayland wandered down the ramp and began walking towards the door, dragging his feet and mumbling to himself, "Here we go again."

Chapter Thirteen

Get it while it's hot

"Slam."

"Aaaargh. Get off me you filthy bastard."

"Robyn?"

"Shut it you, before I blow your dirty face inside out."

"Fair enough."

"Daddy?"

"It's all right sweetheart, daddy won't let the nasty, slimy rapist get you again. Eadrot, grab that piece of shit and stuff him into the air intake on that hyperjet engine."

"Yes sir."

"Bollug, if you touched my daughter it will cost you a testicle."

"No, sir, just startled her when I emerged from the shadows. Isn't that right miss?" Pleaded Bollug.

"Er, yes that's right daddy, no harm done." Robyn lied. Actually he'd grabbed a handful of her left tit, but after the things Wayland had done to it, she would have sounded churlish to be overly bothered.

"Next time, emerge more cautiously."

"Yes sir, more cautiously sir." Phew, he sighed, under his breath of course, ex space paras were meant to be tough.

There was a flash of light in the middle of the hanger, then a muffled, "Ouch." Another ex space para.

"Eadrot? Have you carried out that simple order yet?"

"No sir," replied Eadrot, "It would appear the target has, or had a concealed weapon about his person, which, whilst no longer concealed, seems to have rendered me unable to walk on both legs due to a hole just above my knee which is exuding quantities of smoke."

"Look," shouted Mr Udd, testily, "This shit for brains is emerging and you're exuding. What is the matter with you? I'm not kidding, you just can't get the staff these days. Eadrot, hop over there and bring that living corpse over here. I'll do the job myself."

"Yes sir, sorry sir." There was the sound of a person struggling to get up.

"Daddy? Could I have a word with you? Over here in the light." Asked Robyn. She had dealt with her father for years, and knew pleading wouldn't help Wayland. She knew her father was only impressed by results. She walked over to the patch of light spilling in from outside. Robyn carefully placed her face full in the whitish glow.

"What is it dear, I am rather busy at the moment. If it's about … Your face, what happened to your face? I hope it didn't cost too much, I know plastic surgery is expensive. I suppose the little turd over there took his commission?"

"No daddy, it wasn't a plastic surgeon, Wayland took me somewhere and got me healed. It's all down to him, and it didn't cost a penny."

To his credit, Mr Udd wasn't so stunned to have lost his wits. "Eadrot, cease and desist in the task I have just allotted you. Instead, come here. Bollug, secure the area."

"Yes sir." replied Bollug, then merged once more with the shadows.

"Wayland?" Called Robyn, "You can come out now. Daddy would like a word."

Wayland moved cautiously across the hanger, the laser gun held tightly in his hand. His eyes moved constantly for signs of ambush. A few minutes later he stood a cautious two point six five metres away from the Udds. "Yes, what is it?"

Mr Udd spoke, his voice deep, but low. "It seems my daughter is grateful to you for straightening her face. She has asked me that I reward you in some way for your actions, she also assures me that nothing untoward happened and that you slept on the sofa. Is this true?" He stared gimlet like into Wayland's eyes.

"Yes sir, that is true, I did indeed sleep on the sofa."

"Well, it's a good thing for you that I trust my little girl. When she does lose her virginity, I'll be the one to do it. I mean, I'll be the one to decide who is to do it, understood?

"Yes, no problem." barely stifling a smirk.

"Right. So, here's a cheque for ten thousand pounds, I never want to see you again. If I do you'll wish you were wearing laminated plastic-steel underpants, understand?"

"Yes Mr Udd, completely, thanks for the cheque."

Mr Udd stared at Wayland, snarled, then turned and walked away, dragging Robyn with him. The now upright Eadrot blocked his way until the door clanged, then he slowly limped out.

Wayland was going to ask if he wanted that wound attending to, but thought better of it.

He took a deep breath and stood still for a moment, gathering his thoughts, which took only a few seconds. Then, he leaned over towards the light, looking at the wording on the cheque. It did indeed read, 'ten thousand pounds.' Wayland was gob smacked, bloody hell, he thought, bloody, fucking hell. That steaming pile of mud had earned him ten big ones already. Ten grand! You could buy a really good entertainment system with that. One of those flash ones with the virtual sound, and micro-mini-high-density-blue-laser-multi-layered-read-write-squillion-terabyte-compact-disk players. The ones where you only ever needed to buy one disk, which had everything ever recorded on it. Of course next week you had to buy another CD because it was out of date, but who cared?

Shrugging his shoulders, Wayland walked out of the hanger, looking carefully around as he exited through the main door, just in case Mr Udd had left a sniper to get his cheque back. But all was quiet. Wayland stepped lightly down the street towards the hospital, he was still booked in there for a few more days before he was due back at work, so he was going to make the most of it. Besides he needed the rest, even Mr Stiffy had been quiet all day.

Back in his hospital room he was welcomed by the staff, all clamouring around, wanting to know where he had been.

Of course his bill had been paid in full, so there was no question of him being asked anything too awkward. He explained that he had left urgently to help a sick friend in need. There was a general consensus that this was a wonderful thing to do and they all wished him well for the future. Several of the female nurses and doctors, and one or two of the male ones, gave him their phone numbers. He accepted them all politely, not even thinking that a few months ago he would have run a mile from the male ones.

Quite a few messages had been left for him whilst he was away, and at last one from Honee. She was visiting him later on today, she had something to ask him. Wayland was worried sick about meeting her, he kept thinking he would call her Robyn, like the time he had called Robyn Honee. But she had thought he said honey and had simply replied "Yes, darling."

The bit in the message about 'asking him something' played on his mind too. What if she asked him to marry her? He turned his thoughts quickly away from that one.

The time dragged on, until finally Honee arrived, without fuss or ceremony, simply pushing the door open and gliding in.

"Hello, darling, I've missed you so much. What happened to your hair?" She sat on the edge of the bed and gave him a kiss that went all the way to his todger.

"Oh, it was this scan thing, it all fell off, even down there." Wayland was quite pleased with his smooth lie. He'd been wondering what to tell her.

Honee slipped her hand under the sheets and into the flies on his pyjamas, then cupped his balls. "So it has, Oh and I see he missed me too," she giggled, "perhaps I should get in there with you."

"No," yelled Wayland, a little to loudly, "No, someone might come in, let's wait, I'll be out of here in a day or two. What is it you want to ask me, you know, as you said in your message?"

Honee withdrew her hand, hugged him tight, then sat back. She was all serious and business like now, the lightness of before forgotten. "Well," she began nervously, "You see, I talked to my father about you, he says you have skills that may prove useful. He wants to see you, sort of a job interview." She smiled unsteadily, "We could work together, would you like that?"

"Wow, Honee, that would be good," Wayland was greatly relieved not to have been proposed to and to have remembered her name. "But what sort of thing does he want me to do? I don't know anything about the brewery business. Except for being pissed for a large part of my teenage years, I don't have much experience of alcohol."

"Brewing isn't the only thing my father does, he owns some curry factories, and he's big in sex aids. But I think it's something more down to earth, so to speak, that your talents may be used for." She explained.

"Oh, right, so when does he want to see me?"

"Now, as soon as you can get discharged from here."

Honee squeezed Wayland's thigh comfortingly. "Don't look so worried, daddy won't eat you. Besides, I have a good idea he needs you for something, so the ball will be in your court. Just treat him like the big softy he is, I do."

"I think there's a slight difference between you and me, but I'll give it a go. Let me get dressed and we're out of here."

Just then Fulton appeared, "Here are your clothes, you can go anytime you like, the room's paid for until twelve. Good luck, and let's hope you stay away longer this time, if you know what I mean. Must dash, there's a poker game on in the senior anaesthetists office, and I'm in the pot. See ya." With that the elusive nurse disappeared, never to be seen again.

Wayland looked at the clock, Honee looked at the bed, Wayland looked at Honee, Honee looked at Wayland's crotch. They both smiled, wide, lascivious smiles. Wayland locked the door, Honee ripped off her clothes and stood naked at the foot of the bed. She pointed to the box that controlled the bed, "What does this button do?"

"It tilts the bed." He answered, pulling his pyjamas bottoms over his rapidly inflating dick.

"And what does this button do?" Honee asked, pointing to another button.

"That one moves the top part of the bed upwards." Wayland answered with his mouth full.

"And what about this one?" Honee said, pointing to her clitoris.

Wayland stopped, thought for a moment, then said, "I have absolutely no idea, I'll lick it and see what happens." Honee giggled, then groaned as Wayland went exploring.

Later, they played with the controls, moving each other up and down, side to side, and in and out of course, in various positions, with and without vibrate-massage and heated mattress. The bed's designer, had he been watching, besides having a towering erection, would have been very pleased with the bed's performance and durability. Certainly the last occupant, one Mr Oliphant Junkin, macramé expert and full time tin foil collector, never utilised half as many of the beds built-in features as Wayland and Honee. Well, not in the way these two did. But as the said gentleman was one hundred and fourteen at the time of his occupancy, and was actually, for the majority of the time he spent here, dead, that isn't really a surprise.

Nevertheless, on the stroke of twelve o'clock, Wayland and Honee were both well satisfied, and ready to leave. As they walked through the medical complex and down to the car park, Honee asked Wayland, "What did that nurse mean when he said you should be away longer this time? Have you been away before?"

Wayland had been comparing Robyn's tits to Honee's, giving each a score out of ten for; size, shape, firmness, nipple structure (size, shape, colour, suckability,) presentation and bounce. "What? Oh, er, I don't know, perhaps it was a sort of medical joke, you know, I don't want to see you again because if I do you'll be injured sort of thing." Wayland waffled.

"Yes but he said it as though you'd been away, like whilst you were there. You haven't been in hospital before have you?"

"No, why, were you worried?" Wayland replied, trying to turn the conversation.

"Of course I'm worried about you, I care for you." She blushed slightly, then turned away. "Come on, let's go, dad will be waiting." Wayland sighed with relief, quietly of course.

It seemed Honee wanted for nothing, at least in the way of personal transportation. Wayland was driven to Honee's father's house in a sleek, sporty two-seater, with open top and the latest stealth technology. A present from Mr T'nel for a job well done, apparently. The computer in this one was called Damon, for a reason Honee found amusing, but Wayland couldn't figure out.

The T'nel place was quite modest from the outside, but down right untidy inside. Wayland had passed through the small door expecting some kind of palace. He was disappointed to find it looked like his room back at the main block. "My father was never one for the luxuries of life." Explained Honee. "He would sooner spend his money on a corporate take-over than buy new furniture. He isn't one for tidying either. Get a maid I say. 'A maid? Do you know how much they cost?' Of course, his office is immaculate, all chrome and plastic, marvellous. But that's a business expense he says. And before you ask, no, my place is nothing like this."

Honee led Wayland down a once white now yellow painted corridor. At the end, a narrow, flaking door stood half open, music of some ancient type, Wayland thought it was called Classy or Historical, or something like that, blared loudly. "Dad says we should meet informally first, get to know each other better." Honee pushed the door wider and motioned Wayland through.

He stepped into the room, vowing not to be intimidated by a man who stores his shoes in a plastic dustbin. In one corner, sat in an old leather chair, was a man of middle years, slightly grey, with sharp blue eyes. He was wearing a designer suit, a Masonic tie and had a fresh rose in his button hole. So much for informality, thought Wayland. The man stood, quickly but with style. "Leyland!

Nice to meet you, Honee has told me all about you." He shook hands with the right amount of hand pressure, then gestured Wayland into a seat. "Sit, make yourself at home, we don't stand on ceremony here."

Wayland sat in the indicated spot, a leather chair, but different in style and colour to the other one.

"Dad, his name is Wayland and you know it, so stop playing games." Honee admonished. "Wayland is far too bright for those tricks, aren't you Wayland?"

Wayland just smiled, that was the first time anyone had said he was bright, someone called him a blazing oaf once, but never bright.

Mr T'nel held up his hands, palms out. "All right, no more games. I'm sorry if I offended you Mr Noballs, it won't happen again." He burst out laughing. Wayland smiled again, all this was going right over his head. "No, seriously, let's relax and enjoy each other's company. Wayland, call me Dermot, that's not my name but call it me anyway." He roared with laughter, Honee smiled. Wayland smiled too, but was thinking, 'what a total prat, Honee must take after her mother.'

"His name is Rory, but his friends call him fudge, I don't know why." Said Honee, somewhat impatiently. Her father grimaced slightly then continued. "Right, down to business, my daughter has told me about certain talents you have, but don't worry, I won't tell any one. What you and Honee do is none of my business. No, seriously, she says you can make the sensor vines move to your command. Is this true?"

"Well, I can make them move, to the limit of their root system of course. I don't know about anything else."

"Excellent, a modest man too, but never mind. Could you, for instance, get the vines to move out of the way whilst a structure was built?"

"Yes, I think so, but they'd move back when I stopped."

"Excellent! That's just what I need. Those guys over at D.A.F.T. are a pain in the arse. Can't cut 'em down, can't spray 'em with herbicide, can't block their light. Damn shame, this planet is an ideal spot for a brewery, but you can't get the land, covered in damn plants. The person that controls the land on this planet is the one with all the power, and the person who controls the plants, controls the land, if you get my drift." Mr T'nel looked at Wayland with suddenly penetrating eyes, all hint of frivolity gone.

"Yes, I think I know what you mean, you want me to clear a piece of land so that you can build on it, because the plants are protected and you aren't allowed to mess with them."

"Excellent! A man after my own heart, concise and to the point, not dressed up with flowery language. Yes, precisely. I'll pay you to clear a site and see that it stays clear until the building is up. Then, the vines move back and hide the whole damn thing, perfect! Now, how about ten thou a month, plus expenses and company transport?"

Wayland was gob smacked, he was only getting two thousand pounds as a C.A. plus a shit hole of a room. Actually it had been a decent enough place before Wayland moved in. He tried to speak, to say 'yes please, thank you sir, when do I start.'

Mr T'nel took his hesitation to mean he wasn't impressed. "O.k. I can see you're a skilled man, a talent like yours could well be unique. Twenty thou, plus another five on completion and expenses and the transport. That's my final offer, take it or leave it." He leaned back in his chair, squeaking the faded leather.

"O.k. I'll take it. But just for this one job, any others will have to be re-negotiated." Said Wayland, with far more fluency and confidence than he had formerly shown.

"Excellent! It's a deal, I would have gone to forty thou, but I see you are a man with integrity, I like that one job bit. This works out and word gets around ay? Very smart. Now, Honee fetch the champagne, let's drink to the deal."

Honee stood and walked out of the room smiling broadly, she winked at Wayland as she went out of the door. Wayland was amazed, he never knew he had it in him. It didn't half make him feel horny.

Rory stroked the arm of his chair, "Do you like leather, Wayland? I do, it's lovely stuff, hard wearing, comfortable, very sexy, it even smells nice, a bit like an old woman's cunt." His eyes misted over, as though remembering the very woman. Wayland was shocked, he definitely hoped Honee was like her mother. "Where is Honee's mother?" Wayland asked, as if carrying on the thought. Mr T'nel looked shocked for a moment. At first Wayland thought he had said something wrong, messed up the whole deal.

Then Rory spoke again, quietly, as though pained by the memories. "I had a friend, a dear lady friend, I'd known her for several months, then she died in a freak accident involving a squirrel and a donkey cart. Seems she left me some of her eggs in a fertility clinic. What else could I do? As a gesture to her memory I went to the clinic and had them defrost a couple." Rory leaned forward, conspiratorially, "They put me in a little booth with some blue videos," he whispered, "You know, with titles like 'Girl getting fucked', 'more Girls getting fucked', and 'Getting fucked three'. I was in there for hours, about cranked myself dry by the time I'd filled the vial. I had wrist muscles like a spotty teenager by the time I'd finished. Then the nurse came in and said it wasn't necessary to fill the damn thing, a small amount would have been enough." He leaned back and guffawed loudly. At first Wayland thought the whole thing had been a joke and was about to laugh.

Rory continued, in a voice barely above a whisper. "Anyway, they took the fertilised eggs and put them in a test tube to see if they had taken. One of them was viable, so I rented a womb and nine months later, well eight and a half, you know what Honee's like, out she came. I was so proud, you should have seen her, covered in blood and mucus and shit, she looked terrible. I nearly sent her back, but the midperson said she would clean up nicely. And she did. And here she is the light of my life."

Honee returned with a wooden tray, three mismatched glasses, and a tall green bottle. She placed the tray on an overturned crate. Rory grabbed the bottle, "I love this bit," he said, loosening the wire fastener. Slowly Mr T'nel pushed around the cork until it shot off with a satisfying pop. The cork bounced off the ceiling, hit a stack of folders and ricocheted into a corner, were it probably still lies to this day. He slopped some of the foaming liquid into each of the glasses, then handed them out, largest to himself. He raised it in a toast. "To a future partnership, man to man, woman to man, and as much doinking as you can manage before you get carted away in a box."

"Amen." Agreed Wayland.

"Too right." Honee concurred.

Chapter Fourteen

Creeping Around

"Left a bit."

"Right a bit."

"Back, more, a bit more, o.k. stop."

The surveyor looked over at Wayland, "How long can you keep this up?"

"Er, I don't really know, they won't rush straight back when I stop concentrating. It's more of a gradual thing," answered Wayland. He had arrived at the proposed brewery site this morning, in his new company shuttle, to be met by the surveying team. He had landed, rather well he had thought, on a fallen tree. The surveyors had hiked in from the main settlement about twenty minutes walk away. The area had been smothered by vines, driving out any competition for the available light.

After a few tentative thoughts, moving smaller vines to get warmed up, Wayland had began to seriously think he could murder a pint of real beer. This wasn't too difficult for a man like Wayland, but translating that into 'I need to put a building here to make it' was a little tricky. Finally he had imaged a towering beer glass, as wide as the space needed and reaching to the clouds, filled with brown liquid topped by a creamy head. The very thought made his mouth water, the empathy must have been enormous. Dutifully the sensor vines began to pull aside, rustling and shaking by the kilometre. Less than twenty minutes later most of the area was clear, leaving a lifeless stretch of shallow soil. The surveyors were suitably gobsmacked.

If Wayland's teachers could see now what the power of his brain could accomplish, they would all have wet themselves in fright.

Now, standing around pretending to be keeping the vines at bay, Wayland wondered if he would still get paid if they found out the vines wouldn't return until morning. The team of measurers began to knock posts into the ground, guided by a flickering laser beam being emitted by a small black box on a stick. It was actually the latest planning computer mounted on a monopod, but Wayland was never one for fancy words.

About an hour later the team packed up and moved out, waving to Wayland that he could relax. He made an effort to look like he was coming out of a trance, then walked back to his shuttle.

Well, he thought, that was an easy twenty thousand pounds. The shuttle door opened as he climbed in, "Hello Wayland, I'm so glad you're back, I was getting scared on my own." Said a sultry female voice.

"It's o.k. Ulrika, I'm here now. Let's go back to base, I've finished here."

"Yes Wayland, anything for you," crooned the silky voiced computer, sending a pleasant shiver right down to Mr Stiffy.

Wayland had had the choice of several different personality modules when he collected the one man ship. From the crisply military to the oily slave. Of course he had tried them all, almost going for the dominant female sergeant major, but changing his mind when he heard this one. With a few customisations to the vocabulary she was ready to go.

The shuttle lifted gently into the air, then shot off towards headquarters at maximum speed, Wayland wanted to over fly the surveyors as fast as possible, just to impress them.

In the last few days Wayland had moved up in the world considerably. He had resigned from the flora station, much to everyone's sadness. Sonia and the crew were all sorry to hear he wouldn't be returning, she had a tear in her eye when she spoke on the phone. He had moved in with Honee, she had a flat in a low rise block, which did indeed prove to be better kept than her father's. And now he had been issued with a company shuttle, one of only several dozen on the entire colony, a reflection of the importance attached to his job.

Moving in with Honee had proved the biggest shift. He wasn't used to a girl admitting she knew him, never mind actually letting him move in. The few belongings he had fitted in a small suitcase, but the new salary plus the ten thousand from Robyn's dad went a long way to boosting his collection of junk.

Wayland had also matured a lot, he no longer laughed nervously when he saw packs of sanitary towels, or giggled when he came across pairs of panties. Neither did he feel the need to put any bra he found over his ears and pretend to be a pilot, or to put oranges in the cups. He did have a moment's childishness when he walked in on Honee trimming her minge, but that soon passed.

Honee had also taken him shopping, something he enjoyed immensely. (Mainly because Honee promised to give him a blow job in the changing room.) She picked out some nice clothes for him, which they both liked, and some personal hygiene products, which Honee tactfully said were all the rage these days for young executives. They dined in a popular restaurant he had previously been banned from for vomiting in the manager's cleavage. The large gentleman on the door obviously not recognising him with his new haircut and clothes. When they had finished eating Wayland called for the bill, read it, had a coughing fit he put down to the dry atmosphere, paid the bill and left. He had just spent a month's worth of his previous salary on warm salad and cold meat of tiny proportions.

So, with his new image and flash job title, 'Flora management and control officer', Wayland visited the building site daily to move away any vines that had got in the way of construction. Most days he found the vines where he had left them, requiring only, at the most, half an hour of thinking to clear them away. Even Wayland could manage this, so wasn't overly stretched.

Unknown to Wayland, Rory T'nel had asked many other people to try controlling the vines, even having a go himself. Most could only manage to move the vines a few feet, but even these soon moved back. The vines would move away from heat, cold or physical objects like stonking great bulldozers, but never in a controlled way, and never as spectacularly as when Wayland did it.

One morning about a month later as Wayland was landing in the public spaces on top of the shopping centre, he needed to pick up a new blade for his nose hair clippers, a familiar voice greeted him.

"Hello Wayland, how are you?"

"Robyn! What are you doing here? If your dad wants his money back he's too late … "

"No, Wayland, it's not that, but dad did ask me to talk to you, he would like to see you. He doesn't think he treated you fairly, you know, when you healed my face. If you're free now he'd like to buy you lunch." Robyn said, she seemed friendly, but was very nervous.

"Yeah, sure, why not? Where are we eating? Not 'The Charred Flesh' I hope, I was in there the other day, the food's crap."

"No, he'd like you to meet him in his office, he's laid on a bit of a buffet. Come on, I'll take you." She replied, smiling now, more relaxed.

Wayland, to his credit, didn't make a silly joke out of her last statement. As they walked Wayland examined her face for signs of the scar returning, but found none. He had a dream a few days after their return in which her entire face melted into her breakfast and her father sent a whole squadron of fighter-bombers after him.

"How have you been keeping? I hear you're working for The T'nels now." Robyn asked pleasantly.

"Yes that's right, I've been hired by Mr T'nel to clear some land with my empathic powers." Wayland answered.

"And you've got quite close to his daughter I hear as well." Robyn said with just a trace of sarcasm.

"Oh, yes, we have a flat together, nothing special, it's not the penthouse, just the one underneath," he said tactlessly.

Robyn was quiet for many minutes, until Wayland asked, "And you? Your father keeping you busy?"

"Well, not really, he won't let me do proper work, I get to sit in with the design teams, and he asks my opinion of things, but nothing really meaty. I wish I could work like you, and er, Honee, do something important." She made fists with her hands to emphasise the point.

"Tell you what," Said Wayland brightly, "When I'm rich and have my own business, you can come and work for me." He smiled.

"Thanks." She said tersely.

A small cruiser was waiting to take them across town to Mr Udd's office. When they landed Bollug and Eadrot were waiting.

"Good afternoon sir," said Eadrot, "So we meet again, if I could just touch you all over, make sure you aren't carrying any thing dangerous."

Wayland allowed himself to be searched. "No, sir," smiled Eadrot, "nothing dangerous at all on this one." He and Bollug laughed loudly. Robyn glared at the two, who soon quietened, then lead the way across the roof and into a carpeted lift. This was the first time he had seen carpets in a lift, he was quite impressed. The lift chimed, "Which floor please?"

"Penthouse please, and there's no rush."

"Oh, the penthouse is it?" asked the lift, "I've heard it's quite nice in there, never been of course, I don't get around much nowadays." The lift sounded rather wistful.

The lift door opened half a minute later. "Penthouse!" it announced brightly. A long corridor ran left to right in front of the lift. The same carpet and decorative theme continued along it towards a pair of oak doors. At their approach the doors swung open, revealing a massive office. Robyn led Wayland through the doors then stood aside to let him continue. The office was exactly the opposite of the place Rory inhabited. The outer walls were virtually all glass, some mirrored some smoked, some so clear they looked glass-less. A mahogany desk the size of a small village took up one end of the perfectly square room. Lush purple carpeting blended seamlessly with the linen adorning the walls, which in turn matched the parachute-like ceiling covers. Yellow plastic of the highest quality was counterpointed by shining chrome, and islands of brightly lit red and yellow plant containers, like small forests, were dotted seemingly at random around the place. Very nice, thought Wayland, a man's office.

A metal rod with a looped end descended from the ceiling, passed over Wayland, then retreated. He guessed had just been scanned by a sophisticated arrangement of cancer-inducing rays, and had it found anything one of the men on the roof would no longer be employed, and would have flashed past the window any second.

Two men approached the pair, Mr Udd, tall, grey suit, club tie, youngish, swaggering walk and a barely suppressed urge to rip Wayland's brain out and display it in a cabinet. The other was shorter, though still taller than Wayland, wide, grey suit, club tie, middle aged, and with a barely suppressed urge to hold him down whilst someone ripped his brain out.

"Wayland, so glad you could come," Mr Udd smiled professionally, "Please, come in, make yourself at home. I've ordered a buffet lunch for us, I hope you like Indian food. I love it, all that spice, excellent." Mr Udd placed his hand in the small of Wayland's back and guided him away from Robyn and across to a table so long you could have played cricket on it.

"By the way, this is my associate, Mr Edward."

The wide man held out his hand, "Nice to meet you, please call me Dick, my friends do." He smiled professionally too, gripping Wayland's hand with a number three grip, firm, but not too aggressive at this stage.

"If you'd like to sit here," Udd led Wayland to a seat facing the window, the other two went around the other side and sat facing him. "Please call me Philip, Wayland, now … "

"What about Robyn, isn't she joining us?" Asked Wayland.

"No, not today, she's busy." Philip stiffened visibly when Wayland mentioned her.

"Oh, I thought we were having lunch, as in me, you and Robyn. Perhaps I should be going … " He made to stand up, just to test the water, Robyn had just told him she had nothing to do.

"No, that's fine," Philip said through gritted teeth, "Robyn can join us, I'm sure she can catch up later." He spoke into the air, "have Robyn join us, Jeff, I'm sure there will be plenty to go around."

"Yes Philip, I am certain you are right, I will ask Robyn to return at once." A voice replied from a hidden speaker. Only seconds later Robyn returned, scowling at her father, smiling brightly at Wayland.

Udd stared lasers at Robyn, then said sharply, "Now that we are all here … Jeff, could you tell the caterers we are ready for them now?"

"Yes, Phil, I certainly will, what a good choice you have made. I hear they are very good."

A veritable army of people entered through a small door, dragging portable kitchen equipment with them. The table was soon set with real china plates and silver cutlery. A delicious odour filled the air as the chefs prepared a variety of curries and other Indian food. Wayland's mouth was watering like a tap by the time it was served. Small talk filled in the gap between, mostly by Philip, talking about the weather and colony gossip.

Wayland tucked into a hot bhuna, some vindaloo, and a small portion of biriani, accompanied by pappads and lime pickle. A fiery liqueur of a reddish colour was served with the meal, which Wayland noticed his glass was never empty of. Philip and Dick hardly drank, but Mr Edward joined in the eating whole heartedly.

The remains were cleared away in seconds, leaving not a trace behind except the drips on Wayland's chin. Wait for it, thought Wayland, any second now.

"Wayland," began Mr Udd, "I have heard stories about you, you have a remarkable talent by all accounts, a talent a man in my position could find very useful. It would pay well of course, certainly more than Mr T'nel is paying, and with more perks." He carefully avoided looking at Robyn.

Wayland grinned, he had decided to play with these two, after all what could they offer that he wasn't already getting?

"Well, it's only a party piece really, I don't see how you could make use of it."

Udd and Edward looked at each other, a meaningful glance passed between them. "You are so modest Wayland, I like that in a man, but surely you see the possibilities in what you can do?"

"You mean firing rubber bands at people with just my prick is a sought after skill?"

Udd and Edward looked at each other again, their top lips curling into a snarl. "No, Wayland, I think you've misunderstood. We're talking about the thing you do with the vines. Getting them to move. You know how difficult it is to get permission to cut anything down around here. Hell, I heard of one guy who hung himself and they had to leave him up for three weeks before all the paperwork was finished." Philip and Dick laughed loudly. "His legs had fallen off by the time he was cut down." They laughed again.

"But seriously, even a man of my obvious power has to go through channels to get anything done, if I could offer certain people a service like yours, it would benefit everybody. This colony could certainly use a little expansion, and if we make a little money out of it, so much the better. What do you say?"

"Well, I already do that, for Mr T'nel, why should I work for you?" Wayland sat back and sipped his drink confidently.

"How about a million pounds, per site?" Philip said quietly.

Wayland, not surprisingly, spat liqueur all over the table and Mr Udd. Wayland gathered his wits together whilst Philip wiped himself down with a napkin and tried not to curl his lip in disgust. When he had retrieved some of his composure he smiled slightly at him. "I can judge by your reaction that you are interested by our proposal. Perhaps we could discuss it further?"

Wayland's mind was in a whirl, a-million-pounds ran around, shouting and screaming like a mad man. What-about-Honee chased after him, completely flattening Wayland-slept-with-Marlo as it raced to catch up. Finally, the triumphant smirk and a certain loyalty won out, I won't sell out my friends for money, he thought. "I'll have to think about it, but I'm sure we can come to some arrangement." He said, as calm as he could manage.

Whilst Udd and Edward made polite conversation about future partnerships and investment potential, Wayland went over in his mind the things he could do with a million pounds, if he made the deal of course, which he probably wouldn't. A million pounds was a lot of money, even nowadays. It could buy you a decent house, a car, a good suit and you'd still have enough left to throw the biggest piss-up of your life. And that was for each site! Imagine, every site cleared, new house, big piss-up. Actually that would be better the other way around, one hell of an ear-bleeding, house-wrecking, neighbour-distressing, police-raided, vomit strewn, shag-athon, then move house. Matchless!

Wayland suddenly noticed the room had gone quiet. "Er, sorry, did you say something?" He asked.

Mr Udd smiled knowingly, "I was just wondering how you managed to get my daughter's fine features restored, I am awfully grateful by the way, she's fit to catch the finest of young men now. But she won't tell me, she says I am to ask you. So?"

"Sorry, that's a secret, I don't think I'll ever tell you about that one."

"Really? Well, never mind, it's a pity, because it could be a real money spinner. But as you aren't interested in profit ..."

Udd left the sentence hanging, but Wayland was too slow to realise, and the conversation ceased.

After a round of brandy, synthesised, not the real stuff, nobody in their right mind would have wasted that on Wayland, the meeting came to an end.

"Well, Wayland, it's been nice seeing you, get back to us soon, and if you have any problems, don't hesitate to call Dick here." Udd smiled, gesturing towards Edward with his empty glass. Edward grimaced, managed to turn it into an interested smile, and added, "Yes, anytime day or night, I'm always available."

"Right, I'll do that, see you later."

"Goodbye Wayland, have a pleasant trip home."

Robyn lead Wayland back to the lift and up towards the roof.

"You were quiet in there," Wayland said when they were alone. "I suppose your dad told you not to say anything."

"Well, not in so many words, but he would have been angry if I had said anything out of line, so I just kept quiet. Are you going to accept his offer?" Robyn asked, genuine concern in her voice.

"I doubt it, I wouldn't want to upset Honee or her father. Thanks for keeping quiet about the mud pool by the way, I really appreciate it, I would like to keep that place special, if I can."

"That's a very nice thought, Wayland. Why don't you buy the land it's on? I'm sure the government would let you, they positively leap at chances to off-load some worthless land on people, especially if you could convince them that you don't intend building on it."

"I'd never thought of that, actually buy the land? Who would have thought a Snowball would ever own land?" Wayland's eyes went all dreamy. The lift doors slid open, "Roof! Top of the world! Oh what a lovely view, if only they'd given me mobile optical sensors." enthused the lift.

Robyn stood silently next to Wayland whilst the cruiser warmed up. Eadrot and Bollug stood leaning against the railings, looking smug, grinning inanely. The pilot motioned Wayland over.

"Well, this is it then." Said Wayland leadingly. He wished he could lick her hairless ... No! I'm with Honee now, he thought, I'll have to take her to the mud pool if I want that sort of thing.

"Goodbye Wayland, I hope I'll see you around town again, I'm sure we'll be moving in similar circles now. Goodbye." Robyn turned away, but he was sure he saw a tear in her eye. No, probably just the wind up here. Wayland walked carefully over to the cruiser. When he looked around Robyn had already gone back into the building.

The cruiser dropped him back at his shuttle. He completed his shopping trip, looking longingly in every window he passed, then headed home. He wasn't sure how Honee would react to his meeting, but she was out when he arrived, giving him time to rehearse what he was going to say.

"Honee," he said into the full length mirror, "Mr Udd has offered me one million pounds to clear some land for him. Now, no, let me finish, I know you think I should be loyal to you and your father, but a million pounds is a lot of money, I'm going to take it."

No, that'll sound too sharp, too much of an ultimatum, after all he had only just moved in, he didn't want to be kicked out. But then again, perhaps Robyn would take him in? No, stop it. Get a grip. Wayland composed himself. "Honee, I have had a meeting with a really nice, no, a business acquaintance. He has offered me an awful lot of money to do the same job your father is paying me for. What do you think?" Yes that was more like it, put the ball in her court, and don't tell her the amount.

Chapter Fifteen

Don't worry, I can afford it

"Swipe!"

"Click."

"Whoosh."

Sometime later the door whooshed open, as all the best doors did. Honee entered, smiling, "Hi, Way, how are you?" She rushed over to him and grabbed him by the balls, planting a wet kiss on his lips.

"Yes, I'm fine," he said matter of factly.

"Wayland? What's wrong?" She immediately asked. He was never any good at keeping secrets.

"Er, well there is something, not wrong exactly, more a development." Wayland tried to remain calm in the face of impending doom.

Honee lead him over to a designer settee and sat him down. "O.K. We agreed to share everything and to have no secrets, tell all." Honee sat next to him, an expectant look on her face.

"Well, I had a meeting today ... "

"Who with?"

"With a man by the name of Mr Udd ... "

"The under-secretary for commerce? What did he want?"

"He wanted to make me an offer ... "

"What offer?"

"Honee, you're doing it again, can you just let me finish."

"Sorry, it's a habit, I'm concerned because I love you, it makes me impatient."

You don't want me to describe the next bit, you know what new love is like, all silly pet names and baby talk, yuk! I'll continue about fifteen minutes later …

" … you too, fizzy bum. Now, you were saying, about an offer?"

"Yes. Anyway, this guy Udd offers me some money to clear some sites for him, same as I do for your dad, but at a much better rate."

"Where were you, by the way? How did he find you?"

"Oh, I was just going to do a bit of shopping, you know, in town, he sent his cruiser, big posh job it was."

"Was Robyn there?" Honee asked leadingly, whilst retaining an air of innocence.

"Robin? Who's he?"

"Robyn Udd, Philip Udd's daughter. I think you'd notice if she was, she's quite attractive."

"Not as attractive as you though." Snap! went the trap.

"Oh, so she was there. Did she make you any offers?"

"No, of course not, you know … "

Here we go again. Fast forward, ten minutes later …

" … My little field ration. Now, where were we? How do you know Robyn anyway?" Wayland asked, somewhat worriedly.

"She went to the same school as me, off planet, lower year of course. We met a few times in the gym, she used to be quite good at robo-ball. She was the school's highest scorer the year I left. We've met quite a few times here as well, socially, at parties and such. We get on quite well, if her father gives us the chance, he thinks I'm beneath her of course. I wouldn't say we were best friends or anything, but we have a laugh when we meet."

"Oh." Mumbled Wayland lamely.

"You were telling me about Udd." Prompted Honee.

"Yes. So, after this fantastic Indian meal, cooked fresh on the premises … "

"Flash git." Honee interjected emotionally.

" … He looked at me and said 'We can offer you a million pounds per site … '"

"How much?" Honee spluttered.

"That's exactly what I did, but I had a drink in my mouth at the time. One million pounds, think about it Honee, three or four sites and we can retire comfortably."

"Sod that, make it twenty and retire filthy rich." Honee's eyes lit up, not the reaction Wayland had been expecting.

"Honee, my family have always been poor. A million pounds is filthy rich, I don't think I could manage any more."

"Don't worry, you'll soon get used to it. Come on, we're going to see dad." Honee grabbed his arm and dragged him out of the door, which whooshed closed behind them.

Honee drove, too fast mostly, she was a woman on a mission. All the way across town to Rory's place she kept up a commentary.

"Don't let the way my dad lives or the way he acts fool you. He is a shrewd businessman. If old Udd has recognised your true value you can bet your life my dear father has. If he can get a million pound deal for a quid he'd do it and not feel a pang of guilt. You don't think he pays me that kind of money do you? No, he pays me what I can prove to him I'm worth. Apart from a few extras I wangle out of him with my 'darling daddy I'm so poor' routine. He may be well off, but he's as tight as a dolphin's sphincter, solid even under pressure."

They arrived outside in less than a dozen minutes. "Let me do the talking, we won't settle for any less than seven hundred and fifty thousand. I know that's less than Udd's offer, but my father, despite what I just said, is trustworthy enough to pay up on time."

Wayland watched Honee as she entered her father's abode. He had nothing but admiration for the way she worked, point her at a problem and pull the trigger.

The flat was no better second time around, in fact nothing had been moved. No attempt to clean or tidy the place whatsoever. "Dad?" Shouted Honee, "You in here, lurking in some dark corner."

"I don't lurk my girl, any more of that and you'll go over my knee, you're not to big for a good hiding you know!" Rory appeared from a darkened room, carrying a tray loaded with sandwiches and small bottles.

"Have you got company? We can come back." Wayland stuttered.

"No, just me. Come in, I was expecting you." Rory led the way, passed the room with the leather chairs, into a long dining room. An all glass table dominated the room, leaving little space around the sides. It was at least five metres long, Wayland had forgotten his laser measurer, and two wide, made from a thick slab of clear glass on solid milky glass pedestals.

"Gather around. I thought you'd turn up sooner or later, especially after your little meeting today. Now, we've got poached salmon, peppered beef, or dripping. And help yourselves to the drinks, there's a rather fine old port there somewhere, aged in cargo ships on the slow journey here." Mr T'nel sat at one corner of the table, spreading the bottles and the plate out before him. Wayland and Honee took seats together to his left.

"Dad, how did you know about Wayland's meeting? No, don't answer, I don't think I'd like it." Honee held up her hands, palms out. Rory smiled, biting into a thick sandwich.

"So, if you know why we're here, what's your best offer? And please remember I'm your daughter, so no bullshit."

"O.k." said Rory, swallowing his food. "First, we need to agree an area, acres, hectares, square kilometres. The latter is probably a little too much, for now anyway. The site you've already cleared for us was about three hundred metres by … "

"It was three hundred and eleven metres by two hundred and forty eight." Wayland piped up. "I've got this measuring laser." he explained to their astonished looks.

"Right, so that's shall we say seventy five thousand

square metres. But of course we already agreed a fixed price for that site. For the next one, taking the first as an example, I couldn't pay more than six quid a square metre."

"You will have to do better than that, or we go over to Udd and his bunch of cronies, sorry investors."

"Honee, you cut me to the bone. How could you sell out on your poor father? You know I have a heart complaint." Rory held his hand against his chest.

"Yes, it's missing. Now, fifteen pounds per square metre, or part thereof, or we walk." Honee retorted.

"Fifteen! Do you think I'm made of money? Profits are down girl, all across the board."

"And why? Because there is no expansion. Opening up this planet to careful development would stimulate growth at an amazing rate. With all your different interests you'd be raking it in."

"Why did I ever send you to that expensive school? All right, nine, and that's still too much."

"Ten, not a penny less, plus he keeps all the other benefits."

Mr T'nel sat quietly for a while. He looked at Wayland, then back to Honee, "It's a deal, but only because it's you, and only because you seem to have taken a shine to this young man, lord only knows why." He smiled broadly and held out his hand to Wayland. "Only joking, welcome aboard."

Wayland checked Rory's palm to make sure it was empty, than shook it firmly. He was pretty sure he was happy, but he didn't exactly understand what Honee had got him into, he certainly never knew you could get square metres, long ones yes.

The drinks were passed around, several times. Rory leaned over to Wayland and whispered, "Do you like my table?"

"Yes, it's great."

"Had it specially made you know, when I was younger. The women I've had on this thing, two, three at a time.

Couples too, on it, under it, up against it. The girls love it, bit cold at first, but it soon warms up. You should see some of the videos we made with it, get great views from all angles. Knew a woman once with massive knockers, should have seen them squashed up against the glass. Could have made a fortune selling tickets. Wonder where they went, those videos?" Rory fell silent, apparently deep in thought.

Wayland looked up to see Honee smiling innocently. She mouthed at him, what looked to Wayland like "Burnt them all". Damn, that would have been something to see.

Wayland and Honee staggered out sometime later, the car mumbled under its speaker as it drove them home. They tumbled giggling into bed in a heap of half removed clothing and discovered that Rory was correct, Honee was indeed not too big to be spanked.

The next morning, late morning actually, Wayland rolled out of bed, mainly because he was bursting to pee. Honee was already up and about. "Morning darling," she said brightly, "sleep well?"

"How can you be so cheerful?" Wayland asked quietly.

"Because I'm happy, aren't you? After last night."

"What did we do last night?" Wayland couldn't remember much after turning up at her father's place. After some prompting it finally came to him. "Oh, right the ten whatsits for a rectangle of metres. What was that all about?"

Honee hugged Wayland tight, then hugged him again in case she had missed a bit. "You, my silly little man, will be paid ten pounds for every square metre of land you can clear with that throbbing brain of yours. In other words, one pace that way and one pace that way, and it's ten pounds in the bank. We're going to be rich!"

"You mean, like that piece of carpet there, if it was in the jungle and I cleared it, your father will give me ten quid?" Wayland brightened as Honee nodded. "I can do that easily." He grinned again. "What were you saying about throbbing things?"

Honee smiled and ran her hand down between Wayland's legs, "Oh yes, it is. Well we can soon sort that out." Honee's dressing gown fell to the floor as she sat up on the worktop.

Ah! Young love, doesn't it make you sick?

* * * *

The next few months passed in a haze of sex and alcohol. Apart from the odd trip to the jungle to do a bit of work, as Wayland called it, life was pretty good. He lost count of the numbers of square metres cleared, the sites just got bigger and bigger. Each time he went to a site, the crowds gathered in greater numbers. Many people greeted him by name and shook his hand. "Nice work, Mr Snowball." "Marvellous, business has never been so good, Wayland." "Have you met my daughter, Petunia?" From long ridges cleared for housing developments to huge areas for shopping centres, Wayland moved vines by the kilometre. Not a single other person was able to duplicate his feat. He soon became a minor celebrity.

Honee still went out to do her job, most days anyway. Sometimes they just stayed in bed, decorating each other with squirty cream and chocolate buttons, then licking it all off. The bank balance increased steadily, until one day Wayland checked on it and nearly fainted. "Honee! Look! Some fool has paid millions of pounds into my account." Wayland held the statement out for Honee to read, "It's all right Wayland, it's called income, people get that when they work regularly. Now, as you've got so much, don't you think it's time to start spending it?"

"Yes, that's right, there is something I wanted to buy."

Honee dropped to her knees.

ZZZip.

"Ummmm."

"What was it Wayland, suck, suck, slurp, that you wanted to buy?"

"Ahhh!"

"Gulp."

"A piece of land. Rather a big piece actually, if it's for sale."

"Land? To build us a big house on?" Honee stood, smiling.

"Well, eventually I suppose. Do you remember the place where we first met? I want to buy that."

"Ah, Wayland, you're so romantic, buying the hill where we first made love." Honee hugged him softly.

"No, not just the hill, all of it."

"Wayland! You can't buy the entire range of hills, gasped Honee.

"Why? Is it already sold?" Wayland was disappointed.

"I don't know, but it would cost a fortune. Why not just start with one, then buy the rest later?" suggested Honee.

"Yes o.k. Would your shuttle still have the numbers to find it?" He asked.

"The co-ordinates? Yes, should have, we could go down to the land registry tomorrow, then out to the hill. We could make a weekend of it."

"Yes, that would be great. There is something else I want to show you too, something I found after you left." Mustn't call her Robyn, thought Wayland, concentrate.

The land registry was in a large office in the main headquarters building. Wayland was hoping to bump into Hardstaff, but he was nowhere to be seen. They entered a plush reception area and were greeted by a young man of Adonis-like stature.

"Good morning sir, miss, how may I be of assistance?"

"We would like to buy a piece of land." Said Honee, who had been designated spokesperson.

"Certainly, it's a very popular market at the moment. You will have to see one of our land clerks, s/he will look into your claim. If you'd like to take a seat. Could you also fill in these forms for me while you wait? We operate on a queue system, first in first seen." The Adonis smiled, a bright, white, bleached teeth sort of smile. Honee and Wayland sat down, between a fat man holding a small square of turf and a very tall woman clutching at a leather case with some pressure, and filled in the forms.

It was soon their turn, they were ushered into a large office overlooking the town square. Behind a plastic desk sat a small, weaselly looking man, who smiled mechanically as they entered. "Come in, please, take a seat." He held out his hand for the forms.

Wayland and Honee sat on the two seats opposite the man.

After perusing the forms for a second or two the man spoke. "Now, I will need some form of identification, the exact satellite co-ords of the land and a fifteen percent deposit of the actual land value, plus a handling charge and various other legal fees, as set out in our guide, 'Land and how to buy it', a recommended read, and a bargain at only fifty two ninety nine. Then, if the purchase is approved by the board, we will require the balance of the money and a one off certification fee of two thousand four hundred pounds, or three percent of the purchase price, which ever is the higher, is that clear?"

"Yes." said Honee

"Can you explain the bit about satellites again?" Asked Wayland. Honee gave him a withering look.

"It's all right, Mr?" Honee continued.

"Mr Diddle, Miss. Now, do you have the documents I have requested and a deposit, and of course, first of all, the co-ordinates?"

"Yes, here." Honee handed over a piece of paper with the exact position of the hill on which they met.

Mr Diddle read the numbers. "I am sorry, there must be some mistake, these co-ordinates cover far too large an area for people of your means to afford. What I need is the exact location of the actual ten or twelve square metres you wish to buy." He smiled coldly, handing back the paper.

"No, you will find it all in order. We wish to buy the hill, all of it, with an option to buy the surrounding land at a later date." Honee smiled back, also coldly.

"Miss, Sir, I am a busy man, I don't have time to waste on jokers and dimwits." He looked at Wayland when he said the last part.

Wayland and Honee exchanged a glance, then Wayland stood, hoisted a carrier bag off the floor and tipped three million pounds in thousand pound notes onto Mr Diddle's desk. He sat down with a wide grin stuck to his face, he'd always dreamed of doing that.

Mr Diddle stood motionless for several seconds, "Er, I, er, I just have to go and check a few things, don't go away."

He hurried from the room, thoughts of bank robbery and fraud ringing through his mind. The next room, his main office, contained a computer link to the central accounts department.

Hurriedly he typed in the names of Snowball, Wayland Ulysses, and T'nel, Honee. The names sounded familiar when he typed them in, but he was in too much of a hurry to take more notice.

Honee's details came back, nothing special, no outstanding debts or arrest warrants. Then the screen flashed, a big red box appeared, filling the entire screen;

****

Snowball, Wayland Ulysses. Access Denied.

You do not have sufficient clearance to access this record.

Refer to senior administration officer.

****

"Bugger!" Said Mr Diddle, softly but with a lot of emotion. He had just insulted one of the colony's richest men. He went over to his desk and pulled out a small mirror. For several minutes he practised a real, one hundred per cent genuine smile. Then, lowering his shoulders, stooping his back and rubbing his hands together, he went back into the other office.

"Ah, good you're still here. So sorry to have kept you waiting, Mr Snowball, Miss T'nel. How is your father, by the way, Miss? A remarkable man, sharp as a knife, I've done business with him several times myself. Now, I've checked on the computer, and according to our records that land hasn't as yet had an offer made on it. Also, the estimated value is somewhere in the region of twelve to fifteen million pounds. Which means we would need a non-refundable deposit of about two million pounds. But I see you came prepared, remarkable fore-sight for one so young as your good self." He grinned, trying to make it look real, hoping that they didn't turn hostile. He didn't know what he would do if he lost his job. He had a family to feed, well, a family of tropical fish anyway.

Wayland and Honee smiled at each other, then Honee spoke, her tone icy. "Mr Diddle, you will find three million pounds here, I'm sure that will cover all expenses appertaining to our claim. If you could give me a receipt and a copy of the forms we have filled in, we will be on our way."

"Certainly miss. I'll get those for you right away. And don't worry, I'll see it all goes very smoothly for you."

With the paperwork safely stowed in her bag, Honee and Wayland left the office and went back to the car.

"Wow!" Exclaimed Wayland, "That was great, did you see his face when I emptied the money on the table? He thought we'd nicked it. I bet he crapped himself."

Honee laughed out loud, "Wayland, you have such a way with words."

Inside the car Wayland turned to Honee, "Didn't the thought of all that money and power turn you on? It did me." He glanced into the back seat. Together they dived into the back and began a heavy petting session. When the windows were steamed up enough they both stripped naked and had glorious power sex on the new upholstery. The car, being a top of the range model, discreetly kept the windows fogged, didn't interrupt or peek, and kept the rear suspension rock solid to prevent embarrassing oscillations.

When they had heard nothing further after several days, Honee phoned the office, to be told the claim had gone to special session due to the size and location of that particular land package. Another month went by, again Honee called, to be fobbed off with another 'special session' message. Finally she called into the office herself and demanded to see Mr Diddle. She was told he was on leave and wouldn't be back this side of Christmas. When she asked who was dealing with their purchase, the Adonis receptionist told her a special board had been convened, and they would hear in due course. When she asked who was on this board, the receptionist said he couldn't reveal the names, even if she dropped her knickers and put on a sex show with this telephone.

By now Honee was getting suspicious. She decided to hire an acquaintance of her father's known as 'The Ferret'. A person of unknown description, but documented action. He was particularly good at finding things out that other people didn't want exposed, for a large cash sum of course. The Ferret delivered an envelope a week later. Inside it listed the names of the people on the 'special board'. The fourth name on the list was a Mr Philip Udd.

"I knew it!" Honee exclaimed later. "That dodgy Udd guy is blocking our application because you told him to go and boil his gonads. Of all the sneaky, lowlife, underhand, scum ... "

"Honee, calm down, it's not worth it. It's just another thing going wrong. I've lived with it all my life. I did think it had stopped since I met you, but, it looks like it's back." Wayland answered, philosophically.

"No, Wayland. If you think like that it's bound to happen. Don't let people stomp all over you and blame it on your circumstances, or a family curse, or whatever. If someone kicks you in the nuts get up off the floor and buy an iron jock strap. Next time they won't be so keen. Now, we need a plan of action."

"Yes, dear." Wayland replied. He knew better than to argue with Honee when she was like this.

"O.k. I'm getting an inkling of a plan."

"I thought they were baby inks." interrupted Wayland.

Honee looked at him strangely, not sure whether he was joking or not.

"Sorry, it's something Marlo would have said." He explained.

"Do you miss Marlo? You haven't mentioned him for ages."

"Not miss him exactly, he wasn't really that clo ... good a friend, we just hung around together for a while." Wayland had nearly said 'close' but that brought up memories of 'that night'.

"Anyway. First of all we will have to go and see Mr Udd, find out what he wants. Then, if we can, find a way to counter attack his blocking move."

Honee outlined a plan, filled in some detail and generally planned a winter campaign against the whole Udd clan. Plots of industrial espionage and double dealing floated on the air, thickening the atmosphere to a dark, brooding quiet. Wayland sat back and watched Honee's tits swinging around under her thin T-shirt as she gestured.

After the aforementioned breasts had been well and truly squeezed, sucked, used as hats, and virtually had the nipples licked off, Wayland and Honee finally emerged from under a pile of scatter cushions.

"Can we get on with the plot now?" Honee asked, a broad smile on her face.

"Yes, feel free." Wayland breathed, climbing back into his trousers.

Honee felt free for a while, then they both got dressed. "Right, let's have a word with the slimy toad and see what he wants." Honee grabbed the phone and dialled up the number.

"How do you know the Udd number?" asked Wayland, somewhat in awe.

"Oh, it's just one of the things that guy ferreted out, if you catch my meaning?" Honee smiled, then turned back to the phone. "Mr Udd please, it's Wayland Snowball and

Honee T'nel, he is expecting a call." Honee spoke smoothly, without giving the secretary who answered the phone time to think. A few minutes later Udd appeared, with Dick Edward in the background.

"Ah! Mr Snowball, and you Miss T'nel, how nice to see you. We must meet, we have a lot to discuss. Shall we say eight-thirty at my place?"

Wayland leaned forward to speak but was interrupted by Honee.

"No, Udd, we won't say eight-thirty. We'll say release our land within two days or you will regret messing with us. T'nels aren't to be messed with." Honee cut the connection savagely, but not before watching Udd's face drop like an elderly stripper's cleavage.

"Wha..?" began Wayland.

"You have to tell people you aren't to be messed with. We'll soon have our land when he sees we aren't just little people to be messed around with.

Three days later there was still no sign of the land claim. Honee went straight round to the land office the next morning. She was told by the Adonis front desk clerk that he couldn't find their records, and that she would have to re-apply. The receptionist was quite willing to help her do this if she would come home with him and have sex with his dad, who was feeling a little under the weather. It took some time for the fire and rescue department to remove the yoghurt spoon from his left nostril. He declined to answer questions regarding the incident, but had avowed to himself never to bring a packed lunch to the office again.

All the way home and most of that day Honee fumed, quietly, to herself, loudly to Wayland when he returned from another field trip, and mumblingly in her sleep. That night, Wayland and Honee dreamt similar dreams that involved sensor vines, buckets of soap and long, leather whips. It would be fair to say that the overall tone of the two dreams was somewhat different, but the series of events and props used were strikingly similar. Only the endings differed substantially; Wayland's ended in great, body wracking orgasms, Honee's in body wracking cries of apology. The next morning, they both awoke with smiles on their faces. Honee had a plan, Wayland had a hard-on.

A few days later, anyone who knew Wayland would have seen him hanging around a certain street on the edge of town. Later, another observant person would have seen a man of average height walking through the park, seemingly in deep thought. Meanwhile, a few streets away, three evenings out of four, a couple would walk past a certain boutique in the up-market shopping area known as 'the jungle'. The woman would become deeply interested in the window display, whilst the man would apparently get bored and start to look around.

The next morning, Wayland and Honee were having a lie-in. The tele in their room was on and they were waiting for the news. They didn't have to wait long.

* * * *

"Good morning, I'm Darren Richtoven."

"And I'm Katie Dumblond. Here is the news at ten o'clock."

Darren's teeth flashed milk white as he spoke in his best news reader style "In a 'bazaar' series of events it seems the town of pity is about to be 'reclaimed' by the jungle surrounding it. The home of Mrs Carol Thompson was 'invaded' by so called sensor vines last night. They 'PUSHED' their way in through a 'cat' 'flap' and proceeded to entwine the en-tire kitchen area in thick vines. Luckily Mrs Thompson was 'out' campaigning for Mr Philip Udd's ee-lection to the general council. She has been a 'tireless supporter' of Mr Udd's policies and is seen as the linch-'pin' in his ee-lection drive. We're going over live to the ... Thompson household now."

The scene shifted to what looked like a cubic section of jungle. As the camera pulled back the rest of the house, and Mrs Thompson, came into view. "Well, I don't really know what to say. It's certainly made me think twice about leaving the house unattended. I may have to give up campaigning for that nice Mr Udd. The worst thing is I don't even have a cat."

The camera switched to Katie. Her teeth were just as white, but her boobs were much bigger than Darren's. She had also been having presentation lessons, at her manager's insistence, to increase her saleability. "In another incident, an exclusive boutique on vine street was the victim of a similar invasion. (Smile) The vines entered through a security grill and grew their way through every item of clothing and jewellery on display. (Smile) According to the owner, Ms Jolynn Brass, it appears the jungle is wearing this year's autumn collection before the rest of the colony. (Smile, push out your chest) By strange co-incidence, Ms Brass has been romantically linked to politician Philip Udd. (Smile, look intelligent).

Darren's turn again. He was sure Katie was getting more air-time than him. He had taken to timing her sessions on a stop-watch he kept taped to his ankle. A little practice had enabled him to start and stop it with his big toe, without the viewers noticing. For the last three days running, old plastic tits had been on screen four point one seconds longer than him. So, today he had started leaving small gaps between his sentences. Less than half a second, but enough to make the difference. He expected today's ankle reading to be very satisfying indeed.

"In another vine 'incident', the sta-tue of Prime Minister Allotair in the park by the town square was 'vandalised' by the 'thingz'. Apparently, the green 'thugs' ripped the head from the sta-tue and ree-placed it with an 'ugly' FRUIT. Another vine had 'grown' bet-weeeen the legs of the 'effigy' [Bet you don't know that word, bitch] to resemble a 'large' 'penis'. Several wit-nesses remarked that the 'penis' seemed to gr-ow whenever a horse 'trotted' by. It is interesting to 'note' that Mr Allotair is ree-tiring this year 'and' IS backing Philip Udd in the 'leader' shiprace." Darren smiled again. The teeth had cost a fortune, might as well get my money's worth, he thought.

Katie thrust out her chest for all she was worth, which wasn't a lot as her manager was taking most of the money to feed a growing clotted cream fetish. "And finally, with the local elections coming up, you too can own one of these cute 'Pee-Pee Politicians' (smile). Simply fill with water and amaze your friends as the little figure squirts a jet of water almost three metres (smile). Available in all the major candidates, and available from reception at only ninety nine fifty (smile).

The news credits began to roll, super-imposed on a Philip Udd doll pissing across the studio.

"Well, I would certainly say that will have got the toad's attention." Honee smiled with satisfaction.

"Honee, you are a constant source of wander to me, I don't know what I'd do without you." Wayland misquoted from a cheap soap he'd been watching whilst Honee was out.

"Wayland, you're so sweet, I'm so glad I found you. Let's just lie here and wait for the phone call. Better yet, let's stand up against the wardrobe, I love the cool wood on my arse."

Chapter Sixteen

Ducking and Diving

"Oooooh!"

"Ahhhhh!"

"Buzzzz!"

"Riiiing!"

When the call came it wasn't Philip Udd, it was Robyn. Wayland nearly choked on his own tongue when he saw her, but Honee didn't seem to notice. She was too busy staring at Robyn. Jealous, that's what it is, he thought. It's a good thing she doesn't know there's something to be jealous about.

"Hello Wayland, Honee." Robyn said rather stiffly. "My father has asked me to call. Wayland, my father has a message for you. He says if you don't put right the things you've done immediately, he will inform a certain person about a certain disfigurement and its subsequent removal." Robyn looked pointedly at Honee, a strange look on her face, which was a mix of pity and jealousy, but which Wayland was completely unable to interpret.

"Er, I, no, tell your father that er, I, no … "

"I think what Wayland is trying to say is, we won't be blackmailed, we have nothing to hide. We want our land, and we want it now." Honee regarded Robyn with a look of pity for a second then switched off the phone. Wayland sat with his mouth open, that wasn't at all what he'd been about to say. Shit, he thought, oh shit.

Wayland was in a quandary, he didn't know what one was, but he was in it none the less. Had he thrown everything away for a quick shag or three in a mud hole? What would Honee do when she found out about him and the daughter of the enemy? Would she stop at verbal abuse and leave, or would he be needing a jar to keep his knackers in? He knew Robyn wouldn't be able to take him in, not whilst she was under her fathers control. So he was back on the street, friendless, penniless, all the money was in the land office, in this flat, or in Honee's name. Now, how did that happen?

Honee turned to Wayland, "What was all that about? Disfigurement and removal, do you think it's a threat?"

"I don't think it was a threat, not a physical one anyway. Even Udd can't afford to have dead people turning up on his doorstep. Look, why don't I go over to Robyn's to see if I can sort all this out? I won't be long. Then we can go to the land office and see if our claim has been let through, O.K?"

Wayland stood up, picked up his coat and made for the door. Honee watched him closely. "Wayland, is there something you need to tell me? You seem very keen to see her."

"Who? Her? No, it's Mr Udd I'm going to see, Robyn is just a puppet, she hasn't got a mind of her own."

"You don't want me to come with you then?" Honee asked a little quietly.

"You can come if you want to, but I am a big boy. I think as it was me Udd wanted to sign the deal with in the first place, I should be the one to sort it out."

"Wayland, you're so masterful, come over here and show me how much of a big boy you are."

You don't want to know about the next bit, Wayland just gives her one in the old missionary position.

An hour later Wayland finally got in his car and drove over to the Udd place. He was searched, physically and electronically, then lead into the waiting grin of Mr Udd.

"Ah Wayland, there you are, thought you might drop by. Where's that pretty young lady of your's? Not here, that is a pity. Still, I'm sure she can catch up with the gossip later." Udd leered threateningly.

"What do you want Udd?" Demanded Wayland with more bravado than he thought himself capable.

"Wayland, don't be like that. All I want is to give you a job. Come and work for me and everything will be fine. Loved those tricks you pulled by the way, very amusing, completely ineffective, but it livened up the dull old news programme." Udd walked over to his desk and picked up a sheaf of papers. "Now, just sign these where I've marked them, just standard contracts and stuff, no need to read them." He grinned broadly. Wayland was reminded of a poem about spiders and shit, but he couldn't remember it. He had written a poem once, about a butterfly, he had been suspended from school for it. Ah! Sad days.

"And you're saying if I don't sign, you squeal to Honee about me and Robyn?"

"Well done. I knew you were a bright boy." laughed Udd.

"How did you find out about us, anyway?" Asked Wayland, taking the offered pen.

"I am powerful man, Wayland. I have contacts everywhere. When you asked Robyn to stay for dinner I knew the two of you had been doing more than each other's make-up on your little trip. So, with a little help from the ferret, and others, I pieced together the events of your little have-it-away-day." Udd's fists clenched and his face reddened. "I always swore Robyn would take her cherry to bed with her on her wedding day, and any man who messed with her before then would get a laser-welder vasectomy." Udd stood steaming for a moment, then his face cracked into a false smile. "But I understand that times change, and one must sometimes make sacrifices for one's business. So, no hard feelings, and sign on the line." He leaned closer, to make sure Wayland signed his name, and not someone else's.

"Besides, I've already confronted Robyn with it, she didn't deny it, an honest girl my daughter." Udd added when Wayland didn't start signing.

Wayland sighed. This was all going as he expected. A new twist on the kick-Wayland-in-the-teeth game he had been playing all his life. Now, instead of getting stomped every time he lifted his head, the game had allowed him to stand up and look around, to taste the good life, before kneeing him in the groin and crapping on his head. Wayland leaned on a solid mahogany grand piano and started to sign. He was under no illusions, he had learned a lot recently. These contracts would make Udd a rich man and him a slave, but to have the chance at keeping Honee he had to do it. The pen touched the paper and formed a big 'W'.

"I wouldn't sign those if I was you." A voice called out.

"Robyn!" Exclaimed Wayland.

"Robyn!" Shouted Udd. "Shut up, or you know what will happen."

Udd turned to Wayland, "Sign boy, or by thunder you'll be a hand cranker by tea time."

Wayland groaned softly, why does it always have to be me? He thought.

"Wayland, don't sign. Those contracts tie you up for years. He'll probably tell Honee anyway, just to make you break the terms. Then he'll have your soul." Robyn said, quietly, but with real feeling.

Wayland tensed at the word sole, but relaxed a little when he realised she meant soul. For a minute it had brought back memories of his friend Marlo. Robyn moved towards him, "Besides, I'll vouch for you, tell her it isn't true. Tell her he made it up to get you to sign."

"Robyn! Daughter or not I'll throw you out in a minute. Don't say any more … "

Robyn turned to her father, her eyes lit with inner fires. "Shut up Dad, why don't you go and fuck a duck." She said fiercely.

The effect on Udd was tremendous, he took an enormous breath in, went red, then white. He stumbled backwards, breathed in again, all the while staring in disbelief at Robyn. Philip Udd finally sat down, the breath leaking out through clenched teeth. He sat shaking his head slowly from side to side. All colour and life drained out of him.

"I'll explain later," said Robyn, taking Wayland's elbow. "We had better get you out of here. Don't worry, if my father tries anything let me know, and I'll straighten it with Honee." She smiled, averting her eyes.

"Robyn, why are you doing this? Won't you get into terrible trouble with fat boy in there?" Wayland put his hand on Robyn's shoulder.

"Why? Because I love you Wayland, that's why, but it seems I must do my best to let you be with another woman." Tears ran down Robyn's face. Between sobs she said, "Don't worry about me Wayland, I'll be fine, just don't let Honee down again, or next time I'll tell her myself." She turned away and ran down the corridor. Wayland heard a door slam in the distance. Wayland, like most men, was never any good with a crying woman. He never knew when to slap them for being historical, or start feeling them up to comfort them.

He was escorted off the premises by one of Robyn's robots. As he walked in silence he considered the words she had spoken. She loved him, she had said so. Then why let Honee have him? Strange things women.

* * * *

Things were pretty quiet for the next few months, Wayland went out into the jungles and cleared sites of the ever present sensor vines. Wayland had discovered that there were many slightly different vines, all of which reacted to different thoughts. His favourite, which he called the erection vine, seemed to move towards him when he thought about Honee sitting on his face. He wasn't sure whether the vine was trying to save him from some terrible torture or wanted to join in, but either way it worked.

Soon, he was getting offers from other construction companies, none of which he could accept. But that didn't stop them trying, nor stop them giving him gifts and treating him like royalty. The person in the street was grateful to him too. The colony had become a hive of industry since the land had opened up, creating jobs and stimulating the economy. Best of all, the D.A.F.T. people had given him an award for environmental improvement. The sensor vines grew back over the buildings with a little encouragement, all but hiding the constructions. He had appeared on tele several times and was getting to be quite a hero. There wasn't a place on the colony he couldn't get into if he wanted. From exclusive clubs and packed restaurants, to girl's dormitories and gay bars, there was always a space for 'Mr Snowball and his beautiful lady companion.'

Wayland was going further and further afield now, land occupied by just the vines was becoming rare. Of course the conservationists wouldn't allow any kind of plant to be cut down. So the surveyors got in their shuttles and went looking. One day Wayland announced he was going away for at least three days, to a large island virtually covered in vines. As the isle was surrounded by clear green sea it was planned to develop it as a holiday resort. He promised to save the best spot for a villa for Honee and himself. After a quickie against the front door, yes, they were still at it, Wayland said goodbye.

On the journey out, Wayland was suddenly reminded of Philip Udd. The man had been quiet ever since the meeting, and since the comment about the duck. With a mischievous grin he vowed to get to the bottom of it, not the duck, the mystery. What a headline that would make.

As the shuttle flew out over the greenish shallow waters, it developed an engine fault forcing it to turn back only a quarter of the way there. Wayland, if you believed his version of events, barely escaped with his life, helping to nurse the shuttle back to base through the dark, rain swept night.

Back at the flat, Wayland crept quietly in to avoid waking Honee. He was just about to head for the fridge for a quick chip butty, when he heard a soft moan from the bedroom. Silently, he padded across the landing and peered into the room.

A cold shiver ran down his back as the scene registered on his brain. Honee was on all fours on the bed. Her face, lit by the bedside lamp, was groaning with pleasure. Empty wine bottles lay forgotten on the floor. Meanwhile a figure knelt behind her, thrusting its hips in time to the music playing on the bedroom speakers. The light from the lamp left the other figure in shadow, but looked to be about Honee's height, but slighter of build. Briefly Wayland wondered who he knew like that. A sickening sinking feeling welled up in his stomach. Perhaps he should just back off and leave, Honee had obviously found out about Robyn and him, and was now getting her own back.

He turned to leave, then stopped. No, he thought, no. I've been treated like shit all my life, it's my turn to be angry. I'm going to go in there and kick the crap out of the little twat, and enjoy doing it. He turned back around, flung the door open and switched on the light.

"Wayland!" Gasped Honee.

"Honee!" Shouted Wayland.

"Wayland!" Cried Robyn.

"Robyn?" Queried Wayland.

"Wayland ..." Explained Honee.

"Wayland!" Pleaded Robyn.

"Honee? Robyn?" Wayland puzzled.

"Honee, Robyn!" Enthused Mr Stiffy.

Wayland walked over to the bed and sat down. Robyn detached herself from Honee, revealing a large, strap-on dildo. The three sat on the bed in silence for a while. Wayland picked up a box that had been dropped on the floor, just for something to look at besides the two women.

"The super-firm all rigid vibrating super-penetrator," it read. "Guaranteed to satisfy even the most avid libido. Made from top quality washable plastic in nine different skin tones. Complete with discrete cover for handbag storage. Available in four sizes; Husband (Four inches), Lover (eight inches), Stud (twelve inches), and the special Crowd Pleaser (sixteen inches). Optional extras include; strap-on adapter for ladies fun nights, extra life battery and mains adapter, Kwik-Cleen scrubber for those swinging weekends."

"You know I already knew her, from school?" Honee began quietly. "Well, I rang her to find out how she was, you know, after all the things that have happened. She's moved out of her dad's place you know."

"He told me he would kick me out without a bean," Robyn interjected. "It turns out I was due a large amount of money from my grandfather's estate when I reached eighteen, that tight bastard hadn't told me. It was Jeff who let it slip."

"So," continued Honee, "We got together, rather nervously at first." The two women smiled at each other, tentative but warm. "We decided to meet on neutral territory, somewhere we would both feel at home." Honee's lips curled up in a slight smile.

"That's right, we went shopping." Laughed Robyn. "Then for a few drinks, but I think we had too many, we were trying too hard to relax I think. Then I said something about wishing to see where you lived and we ended up back here."

"We did have a few more drinks as well, and before we knew it we were comparing notes about you." Honee added.

"And, I'm afraid I let slip that I loved you. Honee asked me how I could in such a short space of time, and I blurted out the whole story, about my face and everything." Robyn looked at Wayland, then quickly away.

Wayland gulped, so Honee knows it all now, what happens next? he thought. He looked up, to find Honee looking straight back, a mixed expression of anger and guilt on her face.

"I made the first move," Honee admitted quietly, "I was trying to get my own back for your perceived infidelity."

"And I responded because I thought you might leave her if you knew what she'd done. I was very mixed up." Robyn stopped talking, a bright tear forming on her eye.

"Anyway, that was last night. In the cool of day and almost sober we realised that we liked it, so we did it again." Honee whispered.

Wayland was sitting very still. It seemed strange having the two women he loved here, together. Both naked, with Robyn wearing a large hard-on. He knew if he played his cards right he might be able to hold on to Honee, but say one wrong word and he was likely to loose at least his manhood to two irate women.

"What shall we do now?" Asked Wayland, taking the cowards way out and passing the buck. Honee and Robyn looked at each other, then at Wayland. After a brief, gestured communication, Honee turned to Wayland and smiled. "Why don't you get undressed and lie down, you look a little pale."

Wayland was out of his trousers in record time, his bone leaping out of his pants almost by itself. He laid down on the bed where Honee had made room. Slowly, Honee began to kiss him, starting at the lips and moving down. When she was in position Robyn resumed her thrusting with the dildo, whilst Wayland got blown. Honee groaned as the long plastic shaft slid smoothly in and out. Wayland moaned as Honee's expert tongue and lips sucked and nibbled around his helmet. Robyn sighed, knowing it would soon be her turn to be in between the two.

Later, they did indeed swap around, this time Wayland was behind, thrusting genuine male beef into Robyn, who was bent over with her face buried in Honee's pussy-lips. This time all three were groaning with pleasure, the sound of Honee's orgasm setting off the other two in a cascade of breathy groans.

The next morning they held a democratic meeting. They all talked about their feelings and emotions and what they thought and expected of each other. Even Wayland showed his softer side, getting very tearful at some of the things that were said. The Wayland of last year would never have recognised himself, indeed he would probably have laughed and called him a "soft puff."

At the end of the meeting and several hours later, it had been decided that all three of them would live together, for a while at least, to see how things went. Honee and Robyn made it quite clear that they were a proper threesome, they would do everything together; eat, sleep, live, bonk, shop, everything. If one of the trio was absent, there was to be no sex at all between the other two. Even

Honee and Wayland had to wait for Robyn. Wayland was ecstatic, a dream come true. All he needed now was the power.

The first thing they did together was have a holiday. They disappeared into the mammary hills to visit the hill with the pool and the mud wallow. They spent a glorious month; bathing, eating three-course fruit, exploring, and of course having exceptional, multi-directional sex.

Of course, these things most come to an end, if you'll pardon the pun, the three returned to civilisation, hand in hand in hand. They were smiling like idiots all the way back, with several even sloppier kissy sessions than Wayland and Honee had demonstrated.

On their return, whilst wading through the thousands of E-post, letter, video, audio, multi-media and sky-written messages, they came across one from Philip Udd. Robyn reached for the 'next' button but Honee said "No, it's all right, let's see what he has to say.

Philip Udd appeared on the screen. "Hello, er Robyn? I heard you were staying with Mr Snowball and his charming companion." All three looked at each other, "I wonder what he wants?" they all chorused, and laughed so much they had to rewind the message.

" ... lo, er Robyn? I heard you were staying with Mr Snowball and his charming companion. I was just calling to see how you were. I know we had a bit of a misunderstanding ... "

Robyn snorted, "That's a bit of an understatement."

" ... but I'm sure we can work things out. I admit I was a little hasty, but I was working for your benefit. Call me soon, I'll take you to dinner, anywhere you like. See you soon."

Udd looked off camera, then looked back up again. "By the way, if you're free Wayland, why not come along and see me. I've had a rather interesting offer from a certain high ranking official who needs a new building for his party head quarters. He's picked a prestigious site, but of course it's covered in vines. Might be worth your while going to see him, who knows what favours he could do you in return. No more 'special board' meetings, if you catch my drift." He winked conspiratorially, then blanked the screen.

The trio looked amazed at each other for several moments. "Well, he's certainly changed. Obviously worked out who has all the power around here." Honee said, looking at Wayland.

Chapter Seventeen

Loose Ends

"Beeee-bing"

"Doo, doo, doo."

"Range 200 metres and closing."

A figure came into sight, walking slowly up the long gravel drive. From behind a bomb proof glass window, a laser sight homed in on the figure and locked on, "Missile lock." It said "Fire at will."

"No, it's not Will, it's Marlo, I'd recognise that walk anywhere. Looks like a cross between soiled pants and pissed as a fart." Said Wayland, to the security system. The security system, being very intelligent, and highly paid, simply smiled, electronically.

Wayland jumped into a high powered, fully armoured body suit and ran towards Marlo, smashing the glass to smithereens. The suit pounded the neatly trimmed grass to mud as he sped towards his target. Marlo looked around at the noise, his face widening in terror, "No, Wayland! It's me Marlo Brandon, your friend! Remember?"

"I am a killing machine, I have no friends. Except my mum, but she doesn't count because she is a steel mill." Marlo turned and ran. Wayland trotted effortlessly behind him, then lifted an arm and fired. A small missile burst from the launcher in his wrist and tore towards Marlo. It buried itself in his back, then, after a short delay, exploded. Bits of bloody pink Marlo flopped and drifted in all directions, staining the white gravel and polluting the ornamental fountain.

A quiet, but somehow very audible knock sounded at Wayland's office door. A man entered, flowing into the room, but seemingly not taking up any space, he was dressed all in black, the creases on his trousers as sharp as a Gurka's Kukri. He bowed, "A visitor sir, a Mr Marlo Brandon, he has an appointment. Shall I serve the beer and doughnuts now?"

Wayland switched off the state of the art, full environment games simulator and turned away from the window. Being rich, and a man, he'd felt the need to fill the house with gadgets. Everything from self guided pubic hair trimmers to the most sophisticated whole-house security system. And of course the latest games console, which could take input from any external source and add it to any game. Wayland, Honee and Robyn had spent the last three days solid in a Roman simulation, and they weren't fighting Hannibal.

"Send him in Crawford, and whenever you're ready with the beer and stuff." He just had time to pack away the simulator helmet before Marlo walked in, grinning from ear to ear. He was wearing a beige tank top over a brown polo neck jumper and green corduroy trousers. On his feet were brown leatherette slip-ons with soles 2 inches thick, and he'd had his hair bubble permed specially for the visit. Overall, he looked like a 70's footballer who'd been dressed by his mum.

"Way! Great to see you, nice pad, hear you're living with a bloke and some other woman. Nice, if you like that sort of thing." Marlo leered.

Just like Marlo, he thought, still the same. Unlike himself, who had matured considerably.

"You dick," Wayland snorted. "It's Robyn, not Robin. With a 'Y'. SHE lives here with me and Honee. We've not long moved in. So, how are you?" Wayland was a little self conscious, remembering what the two of them had done in a drunken moment. At least, what Marlo had done, and hopefully because of the drink.

"You sly old dog! Two women, great! Do you shag 'em on alternate nights or both together?"

"Marlo, come and sit down, fancy a beer?" Wayland quickly changed the subject. Marlo would talk about sex all night, typical man!

Crawford wheeled in a chilled trolley on which sat several bottles of beer and a wide selection of doughnuts, then withdrew as quietly as he had appeared.

"So, what are you up to now then Marlo, I hear you're seeing someone." Wayland asked as he handed Marlo a glass of beer. Given the chance, his friend would have drunk the beer straight from the bottle. Wayland tutted inside, some people, so uncouth.

Marlo downed his drink in one, leaving froth on his lip. "Yeah, her names Shelob, after some character in an old book. She works in the Catering Department, gutting fish. And at night she wrestles in beans at the Amorous Axolotl club, it's sort of her hobby. She's a big girl, and not too bright to be honest, face like a cow licking piss off a thistle, but hell she lets me shag her up the..."

"You'll have to bring her over one night, when you're both free." Wayland interjected to maintain what Honee called decorum. "You still in the main warehouse?"

"Yeah, you know, it's ok. Easy money really. I'm about halfway through U, so not much further to go."

"Oh, you're still counting? But Hardstaff told me..."

"No, he's gone, caught him putting pin holes in the flavoured condoms. Trying to get his own back on the bloke who got his mum pregnant or something. We've got a woman now, Variety Foulds, ex porn queen, piss flaps like pigs ears."

"How do you know?" Wayland asked, already suspecting the answer.

"We got all her films out on her first day of course. There're some perks to working in stores you know. You should see some of the stuff they've got in there. You should have seen me when I got to P, I was practically blind for weeks."

And so it went, each telling the other their recent news between glasses of ale and sticky doughnuts. Several drinks later the two of them began to reminisce.

"Do you remember the time we tied condoms to the end of all the air inlets? The offices filled up with latex and spermicide as soon as they switched on the air conditioning." Marlo laughed like a seal on helium. Wayland smiled, was I really that immature?

"I bet you still get a funny taste in your mouth when you see terrapins, I know I do." Marlo laughed louder, slapping the arm of the chair. "Or how about the time when you thought you were the son of Blondini and you tried to walk along the railing outside the dorm? Whoops, one leg one side, one leg the other, right on top of that decorative rivet. How I laughed, I thought you must have lost at least one of your lowballs." He guffawed, unable to talk for several minutes. "Oh dear, happy days, of course that was the day before you left for that plant station thing, heard you got lost whilst you were there."

"Yes, I was misplaced for … What was that, about the railings?" Wayland sat forward, an intense frown on his forehead.

"What? Oh, when you left, remember? No, you were totally shit faced by then. No, you fell off, the railing went right between your legs. If you'd been sober you wouldn't have walked for a week. I bet you had a sore arse when you woke up?"

Wayland reached forward and grabbed Marlo by the shoulders. "Marlo, you are a true friend, have another beer." Relief washed over him, the one fly in the ointment, but it turned out he didn't have sex with Marlo! He fell off a railing whilst doing Blondini impressions. Great! "Marlo, what would you like? Name it and it's yours. New apartment, a job, whatever. Just ask."

Wayland relaxed back into his padded leather chair. Rory was right, nothing like the feel of cool leather. Honee had ridden him like a roller-coaster in this very chair, whilst Robyn pushed the chair around the room.

After Marlo had left, with a fat cheque and a promise to visit again, he sat on the balcony outside his top-floor office. He had three offices in different parts of the house. He didn't actually need any, because all of his business was dealt with by employees. The only thing he ever did was go and move vines and count his money.

With his feet up on an expensive stool, Wayland thought back over his life. He sipped seventeen year old single malt from a solid diamond whiskey glass, nibbled occasionally from a plate of cod and chips he'd had brought here from Earth, and watched as a naked Honee and Robyn played 'dildo wrestling' on the hand woven silk carpet. He had come from an uncouth nobody to a rich, famous, powerful, cultured man, and what's more, he thought, I have done it by myself, with no help from anybody. I have two very sexy, intelligent, good looking women, a house so large I need a map to get to the front door, a car so fast it can actually go into orbit, and so much money it's disgusting. Power? Power comes with the money, no matter what they say, if you have enough readies, you can buy anything. But best of all, whenever he told people his name, the few who didn't already know, instead of laughing, or hiding a laugh, they were awed, humbled. The name Snowball was now mentioned in hushed tones, not stifled giggles.

He farted loudly, lifting up his cheek for maximum volume. An unobtrusive robot extended a small tube and sucked away the offending odour before it was even cold.

A broad smile lit up Wayland's face. A fart catching automaton, now that's what you call style!

The End

Appendix

Extract from the "Encyclopaedia of Everything"

Snowball. A roughly spherical ball of compacted snow made by children and adults alike for projectiles during winter recreation.

Two. 'To snowball.' To grow exponentially in size.

Three. 'A Snowball Promotion.' To rise to great fame and wealth through hard work and sacrifice.

Pratts People, Page sixteen hundred and two

SNOWBALL, Wayland U. Business tycoon and philanthropist. Discoverer of 'Cellular-matrix-morphotic compound' widely used in the treatment of burns. Discoverer of 'empathy-induced-taste-impression fruit' a popular food native to his planet, Greenshy. Rose to power after developing a so far unique talent for empathic motivation of a family of semi-mobile vines native to Greenshy. The first person in history to own an entire planet. Winner of the charity foundation 'contributor of the year award' for the last twelve years. Attributed with near total recall. Discoverer of the only alien artefact ever found by man, a spherical object buried in a cave in a secret location on Greenshy.

Galactic Gardens, An article on 'Snowballia Waylandii' and other Greenshy natives

Snowballia Waylandii

This easy to cultivate family of vines comes in a variety of sizes to suit most gardens...

… But don't expect to be able to move it around, only the great mind of Sir Wayland Snowball can do that!

Greenshyia Snowballii
A low growing, odiferous shrub. Adaptable, slightly acidic nectar, propeller shaped flowers. Discovered by Sir Wayland Snowball. The story goes …

Triagustia Snowballii, fa 'Ulysses'
The fruits of this bush are quite remarkable … seem to take on different flavours …

Mrs Dribbles 1,000,001 favourite recipes. Snowball Steaks
Take a few two pound steaks, preferably Earth grown …

Wayland's School Work, Creative Writing

A Poem, "The butterfly'
by Wayland Snowball, aged twelve.

A butterfly fluttered by, on a summer's day.
It flittered past my window, then it went away.

A butterfly fluttered by, skipping around my room.
Its lovely colours brightened my heart and chased away the gloom.

A butterfly fluttered by the next day after that.
I wish it would just piss off, the cheerful little twat.

(Suspended, two weeks).

A Song, 'Down to the zoo'
by Wayland Snowball, aged fourteen.

I love her, you know, but what can I do?
She lives in a paddock, down at the zoo.
She's warm and cuddly, someone named her Deborah.
She's black and she's white and I think she's a Zebra.

Chorus

Frilicky frolicky rolicky roo.
The things I get up to when I'm down at the zoo.

So here I go with my carrots and crate.
Over the fence and in through the gate.
That large four legged shape so sexy to me.
I drop my trousers and smile with glee.

Chorus

I put all the carrots in her nose bag.
Then I nip round the back with my crate for a shag.
You say I'm sick, do I hear you whine.
But you've never had sex 'til you've had equine

Chorus

If I take grass and rub it on my dick.
She'll suck it and suck it and give it a lick.
Of her tongue and her lips I am so glad.
She's the best blow job that I've ever had.

Chorus

Someone has told me this past week or two.
They moved my young Deborah to another zoo.
I've rubbed it and scrubbed it and bleached it of course.
But for the last week I've been shagging Hector the horse.

Frilicky frolicky rolicky roo.
The diseases I've caught whilst down at the zoo.

(Expelled)